"IT SEEMS YOUR ALIBI IS ABOUT AS AIRTIGHT AS MINE, Agent Donovan."

He spread his hands wide. "But what motive would I have?"

Kat angled her head at him. "Money?"

"I don't need it."

She thought about the remarks he'd made concerning the letter's owner, Lady Mercer. "Love?"

James's brown eyes widened, then he shook his head with deliberate slowness. "Not in my vocabulary."

Intrigued, Kat filed away his response. "Just for the thrill of it?"

He caught her gaze, then leaned forward on his stool until his face was only inches from hers.

Kat froze, unable to look away, appalled at her thrashing heart. The man's senses were so superhuman, he could probably hear it.

His eyes sparkled with warmth and humor, and his mouth was drawn back, revealing both dimples. His breath feathered across her chin three times before he smiled and said, "I'd rather get my thrills taking things which are freely given."

Her pulse and the music from the stereo pounded in her ears. Her throat constricted, forcing her to swallow, painfully and audibly.

He reached forward in slow motion until he touched her cheek with his warm forefinger. Kat's eyes closed involuntarily, her mind spun, her lips opened a fraction.

"You," he whispered, "look good enough to eat."

WHAT ARE *LOVESWEPT* ROMANCES?

They are stories of true romance and touching emotion. We believe those two very important ingredients are constants in our highly sensual and very believable stories in the LOVE-SWEPT line. Our goal is to give you, the reader, stories of consistently high quality that may sometimes make you laugh, sometimes make you cry, but are always fresh and creative and contain many delightful surprises within their pages.

Most romance fans read an enormous number of books. Those they truly love, they keep. Others may be traded with friends and soon forgotten. We hope that each LOVESWEPT romance will be a treasure—a "keeper." We will always try to publish

LOVE STORIES YOU'LL NEVER FORGET
BY AUTHORS YOU'LL ALWAYS REMEMBER

The Editors

LICENSE
TO
THRILL

STEPHANIE
BANCROFT

BANTAM BOOKS
NEW YORK · TORONTO · LONDON · SYDNEY · AUCKLAND

LICENSE TO THRILL

A Bantam Book / October 1997

ISBN 0-553-44575-8

Published simultaneously in the United States and Canada

PRINTED IN THE UNITED STATES OF AMERICA

OPM   10 9 8 7 6 5 4 3 2 1

To Ruth Kagle,
a consummate professional
and a jolly good friend

PROLOGUE

Surrey, England

"James, darling, I knew you would come." The stunning blonde set a champagne glass on a small marble table and gracefully rose to her feet.

James Donovan strolled into Lady Tania Mercer's sitting room and lowered a friendly kiss onto her raised red mouth. "I've never been able to refuse you, Tania," he said smoothly.

"Almost never," she corrected him, then smiled languidly. "I'm afraid this favor will be a bit more arduous than a night in my bed, James."

He grinned. "My lady, I doubt if even the British government could have manufactured an assignment *that* harrowing."

Tania scoffed prettily and offered him a drink. While she mixed him a martini, James studied his former lover. Their brief affair had ended more than five years ago, before he retired from the British Secret Service. Tania had been a pleasant diversion from his unpredictable and often dangerous job. She'd wanted more than he could offer her, more than he could offer any woman, but they'd parted on congenial terms.

Lady Mercer moved in interesting circles and always had her finger in mysterious pies, so whatever the "favor," he had a feeling it would be more entertaining than hunting and gaming on his estate, which had grown tiresome of late. "I have to admit your invitation has piqued my curiosity."

She handed him his drink and laughed, a tinkling sound. "I figured after six months of inactivity, you might be getting restless."

James pursed his lips to suppress a smile. "I haven't been *completely* immobile."

She raised a finely arched brow. "I was referring to your daytime activities, James."

He raised his glass toward her. "You know me well, Tania."

She inclined her head in agreement, touching her glass to his before taking a sip. "What would you say to a business trip to the States?"

He angled his head, surprised. "I've actually been toying with the idea of an extended holiday in New York City."

"Unfortunately, this job would take you to the West Coast, to San Francisco."

Nodding agreeably, he said, "I can combine the trips. What exactly did you have in mind?"

She swirled the liquid in her glass and shrugged. "It's really quite mundane compared to your usual exploits, I'm sure, but I need an armed guard to accompany a courier and a piece of art to a museum there."

James laughed. "Are you dabbling in fine arts now?"

"It's a letter, actually. A very old letter which recently

came into my possession. I have reason to believe it is extremely valuable."

"It sounds like a simple enough job," James said. "Why do you need me?"

Her mouth formed a lovely pout. "I need someone I can trust, and to be honest, I'd hoped we might be able to pick up where we left off once you returned."

But James's mind was elsewhere. In truth, her request had come at a good time. He'd been asked to consult on a case of improprieties at a London museum and had declined because his knowledge of the industry was so slim. This trip would allow him to pick the brain of a trained courier and perhaps he could offer assistance upon his return from New York.

Tania stood and slid her hand down the front of his linen shirt. "I could join you in the States once I've settled my affairs here. I love New York this time of the year, and I've missed you, James."

He accepted her full-body kiss with only a mild stirring, a fact that irritated him. He was obviously losing his edge if he could conjure up so little interest in such a beautiful and skillful lover as Tania.

Apparently his lackluster response did not go unnoticed. She drew back, a frown marring her perfect brow. "Have you found a serious love interest?"

"No," he said rather sharply, then laughed. "You forget who you are talking to, my dear."

She sighed dramatically. "I see you are still enjoying your reputation as untouchable, James."

"Well," he murmured, dipping his head to hers again, "I wouldn't go quite that far."

ONE

"Testosterone," Kat McKray said, viciously squeezing a dribble of juice from the lemon wedge into her water glass. "Testosterone is the root of the world's problems."

"MMMMnnnn," her best friend, Denise Womack, agreed as she sipped her tea.

"Overbearing men, everywhere I turn." Kat pounded her fist on the café table. A waiter who had stopped to refill their drinks eyed her warily and moved on. She pushed her wire-rimmed glasses higher on her nose. "If you ask me, hormone therapy would be the quickest route to global peace."

Denise swallowed and arched an overplucked eyebrow. "Speaking of hormones, Kat, yours are running a bit high today." Then she squinted and nodded knowingly. "You need a man."

Kat's mouth fell open. "You're delirious—that's the last thing I need!"

But her red-haired friend only grinned. "You, my friend, are horny."

Flustered, Kat could only gasp in outrage. "That's

ridiculous—just because I've had it up to my eyeballs with pushy men, doesn't mean I'm . . . anything."

"Let me guess—Napoleon's being a pain in the ass again?"

"Again? He didn't stop long enough to *resume*."

"So why do you put up with the little dictator? He couldn't run the museum without you."

Kat sighed and tore off a chunk of buttered roll. Her friend didn't know it, but she was planning her escape in two months, she just hadn't yet chosen a destination. "I've been giving serious thought to leaving Jellico's."

"There are dozens of museums and galleries in San Francisco alone that would pluck you up in a minute!" Her friend popped a cherry tomato into her mouth for emphasis.

Kat cupped her hand behind her ear and tilted her head.

"What are you doing?"

"Listening as my father turns over in his grave for me even thinking about leaving Jellico's."

After a wry laugh, Denise said, "You've already made your mark there—why else would they have chosen you to handle the showing of the king's letter?"

"*Alleged* king's letter," Kat said. "It hasn't been authenticated yet. And this is a prime example of my boss lowering the standards of the museum by agreeing to show a document that might not even be genuine."

"I saw an interview with the owner on the national news last night—she's convinced it's real."

Kat laughed. "Lady Mercer has a vested interest in spreading that rumor—American collectors are clamoring for an invitation to bid on the letter."

"She'll be rich."

Nodding, Kat added, "*If* it's genuine."

"What do you think?"

Kat chewed her bread, then said, "I think it's highly suspicious when a two-hundred-year-old historically significant document suddenly appears."

"The news segment said the letter has been hidden between the pages of an old book and packed away in a trunk."

Pursing her lips, Kat shook her head. "Seems a little pat to me."

"It happens, doesn't it?"

"Sure," Kat conceded with a shrug. "It hasn't been so long since that art collector attended a party and noticed a Michelangelo statue on a pedestal in the host's home. The piece was simply a fixture when they purchased the house, and the owners had no idea of its worth."

"Wow," Denise said, her eyes shining. "And now a love letter from King George III has come to light—you have to admit it's kind of romantic, Kat."

"*If* it was written by King George III," Kat said wryly. "Besides, I think the collectors are more interested in the part about him being sympathetic to the American Revolutionaries than about the naughty talk to a mistress."

"Have you read it?"

"No," Kat said. "I just know what the newspapers are reporting, same as you."

"Imagine, something worth so much money sitting right under your nose. Wouldn't it be great if that hideous gargoyle on my fireplace mantel turned out to be worth something? Of course, it wouldn't have to be a mint—I'd settle for a measly thirty-five thousand, two hundred and fifty dollars."

"Still trying to find a way to buy your condo?" Kat asked sympathetically.

Denise nodded. "I've got six weeks to come up with the down payment or I'll have to move."

"Got any rich relatives?"

"Not any on the verge of dying, unfortunately."

"You could marry my boss," Kat suggested cheerfully. "And then get him off my back."

Denise made a face. "I'm not getting on *my* back to save yours."

"And why risk making that new boyfriend jealous?"

"Kat, I keep telling you, this guy is just a friend."

"So what's his name and when will I meet him?"

"Never mind, okay? What time does the letter arrive?"

Kat grinned and pointed her fork at her friend. "I could tell you, but then I'd have to shoot you."

"I only asked because I need to borrow your washer and dryer tonight."

"Again? As much as your appliances break down, I'd think you'd be glad to move."

Denise adopted a drawl. "It ain't perfect, but it's home."

Kat squinted, mentally moving through the remainder of her day. "Besides the arrival of the infamous love letter, I have to develop a schedule to inventory our vaults. Arrrgh! I'm glad it only comes once every three years—I'd rather have a mammogram."

Denise eyed her friend's large breasts and ran a hand over her own flat chest. "Ouch."

Kat laughed. "I should be home by seven o'clock."

"Thanks." Her petite friend flagged the waitress, then plopped down a couple of bills and some change.

"See you tonight," she said, then waved and scampered off.

Kat watched her retreat, noticing several male heads turn. She scanned Denise's picked-over salad, then frowned and glanced down at her own plate of fettuccini Alfredo. "I'm starting a diet," she murmured, then twirled the noodles onto her fork. "Tomorrow."

But as she walked back to the museum, Kat pushed aside thoughts of her snug waistband. The manuscript would arrive by courier from London around three o'clock. Upon arrival, she and the courier would note the condition of the document, then place it in the vault for the evening, where it would await the ministrations of a team of international experts on eighteenth-century British manuscripts.

Sending the letter to the States had been a brilliant move on the part of the owner, she noted. Most British historians had been outraged at the supposed content of the letter, and, naturally, most American historians had been delighted. The letter would make its debut next week at Jellico's, San Francisco's most renowned private museum and gallery.

As she badged in at the rear staff entrance, Kat laughed to herself, wondering if George would be amused at the new little war he'd started between England and the United States. Her smile dissolved when she saw her boss, Guy Trent, standing two feet inside the door, arms crossed, toe tapping.

"Where have you been?" the short man barked.

Kat adopted her own authoritative stance—not too difficult considering she towered over him by a good six inches. "To lunch," she retorted.

She didn't miss his gaze flitting over her unfashionably round figure. The immaculately dressed middle-aged man sniffed, then drew himself up. "Well, while you were having *lunch*," he said as if she'd committed a grievous sin, "the courier arrived."

Kat's pulse jumped. "I wasn't expecting him for another two hours."

Frowning, her boss walked to another door and flashed his badge in front of the card reader. "They're waiting in the painting vault with Andy."

"They?" She rushed to keep up with him as he trotted down the hallway.

He looked at her as if she were half-witted. "The courier and the armed guard."

Now it was Kat's turn to frown. She mentally scanned the details of the Mercer deal as they stopped before the door of the vault room and signed in at the guard's desk. "There was no mention of an armed guard in our negotiations."

Guy flashed his badge again, and the light over the doorknob blinked. Placing his hand on the knob, her boss said, "Tell that to Her Majesty's secret service man."

Kat frowned, then lightly patted her tight chignon, even though she knew every dark hair was in place, as usual. She gave her black crepe suit a quick glance and smoothed a hand over her hips, sending the hem of her long skirt swishing around her ankles as she followed her boss into the vault.

The temperature- and moisture-controlled room was lined with narrow metal cages fitted with handles to slide them from their respective slots. Each cage was designed to hold a separate piece of art—in this particular vault, paintings, and in some cases, documents.

Two men stood beside her co-worker Andy Wharton, and Kat's eyes were instantly drawn to one of the strangers. Dressed in a slate-gray Armani suit, the dark-haired man stood well over six feet tall, his brown eyes squinting slightly as he sized her up in return. Tiny hairs rose on the exposed nape of her neck. The slight bulge of a shoulder holster beneath the fabric of his breast pocket confirmed his position, but this man was no rental cop.

"Gentlemen," Guy said, smiling grandly. "May I present the curator who will be handling the letter, Ms. Katherine McKray. Kat, this is Mr. Muldoon, the courier."

Kat dragged her eyes from the tall stranger to offer her hand and a smile to a smaller, wiry man. Mr. Muldoon nervously relinquished his grasp on the letter transport box just long enough to give her a two-finger handshake.

Guy swept his hand up and toward the larger man. "And this is Mr.—"

"Donovan," the man supplied, his English accent lazy and rumbling. The right side of his mouth lifted as he captured Kat's gaze and held it. "*James* Donovan." As he spoke, a dimple appeared, then disappeared.

Awareness of the man's blatant sex appeal skittered over her nerve endings as she clasped the roomy hand he offered her. "How do you do, Mr. Donovan."

The left side of his mouth joined the right, resulting in a devastating smile. "At the moment, Ms. McKray, I'm quite charmed, thank you."

His rich, velvety accent cloaked her eardrums. Was there anything more sexy in all the world? His fingers were long and well-shaped, warm and strong. When it seemed he had no intention of releasing her hand, she withdrew it carefully, mindful of the friction between their palms.

"You've taken us by surprise, gentlemen," she said,

rubbing her violated hand and purposely turning her attention to Mr. Muldoon.

The thin man shifted nervously, then slid his gaze to his companion. "It was Mr. Donovan's idea."

Feeling like a spectator at a tennis match, she looked back to Mr. Donovan, who was now leaning casually against a table, one hand in the pocket of trousers that looked incredibly wrinkle free considering the arduous flight. The man shrugged. "I thought it would be safer to arrive early in case you had notified a television crew."

Kat kept her tone cool. "Mr. Donovan, we're not in the habit of inviting news crews to film our security measures." The raising of one thick eyebrow was his only response, so she continued. "While we're on the subject, *we* should have been notified that a guard was traveling with the letter. Since you share our security concerns, I'm sure you'll understand why we'll need to contact Lady Mercer to verify your credentials."

His eyes glinted in open amusement. "I've no doubt Lady Mercer will give me . . . *glowing* marks."

Kat bit the inside of her cheek to minimize her reaction to his thinly veiled innuendo. "Even so, payment for an armed guard was not in our contract."

"That's fortunate," he said, adopting a serious expression and crossing his arms. "Because you couldn't afford me."

Guy cleared his throat and stepped forward. "I'm sure we can work this out," he said pleasantly, then sent a reprimanding glare toward Kat.

Andy Wharton, the ponytailed painting restorer, made a shuffling sound with his feet. "I'll make the call," he said, then left the room hurriedly. Undoubtedly to escape the presence of the arrogant Mr. Donovan, Kat thought.

She narrowed her eyes at the British man. "Just what exactly do you do for a living, Mr. Donovan?"

"I'm retired from the government's employ, Ms. McKray. I'm going to New York City on holiday, and Lady Mercer's request to accompany the letter came at a convenient time."

"New York by way of San Francisco sounds a little inconvenient to me for such a short meeting."

He winked. "I could be persuaded to stay a fortnight or two."

Kat bristled and opened her mouth, but Guy cut in, addressing Mr. Muldoon loudly. "Well, I can't tell you how delighted we are to be showing the letter."

"So nice you could accommodate us on such short notice," the courier said, his clippish voice slightly nasal.

Guy beamed and Kat forced a smile—her boss knew she was less than enthusiastic about showing the piece. She kept her voice cordial. "I try to remain flexible, Mr. Muldoon."

"Which, if I may say so, is a most desirable quality," James Donovan interjected.

Kat jerked her head toward him, but his eyes were wide and innocent.

"We're expecting large crowds," Guy continued, glazing over the moment.

James Donovan sighed. "Mr. Trent, my companion and I are a bit whacked from the trip. Can we, as you Americans say, get the show on the road?"

Guy started to nod, but Kat stepped in. "Not until we've spoken to Lady Mercer."

On cue, a buzz and click sounded, and Andy reentered. "She said Mr. Donovan is a close friend of hers who agreed to accompany the courier."

"Very well," Kat said, avoiding the eyes of the man

they were discussing. "Then let's open the box and see what all the fuss is about, shall we?"

Mr. Muldoon broke the outer seal of the container. Andy passed out latex gloves, and everyone watched as the lid was lifted and the special packing paper moved aside to reveal three small sheets of yellowed parchment. Kat lifted the plastic-encased sheets and placed them side by side on a table. Since the letter was written in nearly illegible German, a translation sheet had also been provided, along with a disclaimer, noting contemporary interpretations and conjecture concerning the indiscernible passages.

"Read the translation," Andy urged, craning for a view.

Kat squinted at the sheet. "It's undated. 'Dear Madam, I am penning you this note since I must once again break our regular engagement. It seems the goings-on in the world are determined to encroach on our private time, yet another reason to detest the trappings of my title. But if I could feed at'"—she cleared her throat and forged ahead—"'But if I could feed at thy youthful breast as a commoner, I would be a satisfied man. Instead I must deal with those who are bent on sending me to an early grave with their infighting. The bawdy Americans are a thorn in my side, but I admire their audacity and envy their freedom in that virgin frontier. I tire of the wars and wish I would discover a dignified end. Until I can lie beside thee again, keep me in thy heart.'"

"What do you think, Kat?" Andy asked, his pale eyes wide.

Still peering at the sheets, Kat shook her head. "This is not my area of expertise, Andy, but the man had serious bouts with insanity." She glanced up at Mr. Muldoon. "Do you have the conditioning sheet?"

He nodded and withdrew the documents from an inside jacket pocket. With the aid of a magnifying glass, he and Kat went over the documents inch by inch and recorded all imperfections, as was required with each incoming piece. By the time they were finished, her back and neck hurt from bending over the letter, and her watch read four o'clock.

She stepped back and massaged her aching shoulder, stiffening when she felt someone watching her. James Donovan had been so quiet while they had studied the letter, she'd hoped he'd fallen asleep. But instead he was suddenly right behind her.

"May I lend a hand?" he asked, his mouth near her ear.

She stepped forward. "No, thank you," she said coolly.

"Watching you work I couldn't help but wonder if under that nun's skirt is a beautiful pair of legs to match those exquisite ankles."

Anger, coupled with the hum of desire, struck low in her stomach. Kat closed her eyes and cursed under her breath. Denise had been right—sixteen months without a man was obviously getting to her if such a pathetically blatant come-on had the ability to stir her. But she was not about to give this man, who was apparently used to women falling at his expensively clad feet, the satisfaction of a swooning response.

She turned to him with her brightest smile, but faltered a bit when the impact of his handsome, angular face struck her anew. His nose and brow were prominent, his eyes shone like black glass. Inhaling deeply, she was careful to keep her tone out of hearing range for the other men in the room. "For your information, Mr. Donovan, my legs *are* beautiful. Such a pity you'll never see them."

A small frown creased his brow. "I see—you prefer women."

Kat blinked. "Excuse me?"

He sighed. "Which some men find intriguing, but not I, I'm afraid."

Pursing her lips in frustration, Kat said evenly, "I don't prefer women, Mr. Donovan, I just don't prefer you."

"I'm an acquired taste," he assured her, displaying one dimple, "but addictive. Would you join me for supper? My flight doesn't leave until eleven o'clock."

She had to admit, it sounded more appealing than sharing a pizza with Denise while her friend did laundry. But this man's arrogance alarmed her because, well . . . his arrogance might be warranted. "I already have plans."

"To curl up with a cozy book?" he asked, his voice teasing.

"No," she retorted, irritated he'd come so close to the boring truth.

"Careful with that temper," he warned, raising a finger. "You might pop your bun loose."

"Kat," Guy said from across the room. "We're ready to catalog the letter."

Grateful for the interruption, Kat swept past James Donovan and turned her attention to the letter. Once the document had been placed in another environment-controlled container, it was inserted into one of the cages, then slid back into the wall among the other cages—where it would stay until the scientists trickled in tomorrow.

"Mr. Trent gave me a tour of your laboratory," Mr. Muldoon said to Kat as they left the vault. "I'm most impressed."

She smiled, genuinely pleased. "Thank you—we're very proud of our new restoration facility." The project had been her father's brainchild over a decade ago, before she'd come to work at Jellico's under his tutelage. He'd died in a car accident only a few weeks before the lab was operational. His face rose in her mind and tears pricked her eyelids, but she quickly blinked them away.

After they signed out, Kat extended her hand to Mr. Muldoon. "Good-bye, Mr. Muldoon," she said warmly, and while the others were exchanging small talk, Kat turned to James Donovan. "I hope you enjoy your stay in the States, Mr. Donovan."

"I would like to meet your head of security to discuss a few issues before I leave."

Kat's laugh was short and dry. "Mr. Donovan, certainly you don't expect me to give you the run of my museum."

"No," he said pleasantly. "Just standard precautions, I assure you."

She pursed her lips. "Sir, our painting vault contains many valuable works—some worth much more than a letter which has yet to be authenticated. We typically don't give security demonstrations."

"I'm wounded you don't trust me, Ms. McKray. I can arrange for associates from the FBI and the CIA to contact you within the hour to vouch for my good character."

Kat frowned. "From what organization did you retire, Mr. Donovan?"

"I was an intelligence agent for the British government."

"Agent double-oh-seven?" she scoffed.

"No," he said in a grave tone, then leaned forward and whispered, "Agent sixty-nine." His mouth bent in a lopsided smile that left her wondering if he was struggling not to laugh at her.

That smile of his still mocked her when she unlocked the door to her apartment after work. She glanced at her watch. Six-thirty. Denise would be here soon, and they would settle in for several hours of female bonding over beer and pepperoni pizza. Kat yawned widely at the prospect.

As she undressed and rehung her suit, she felt twinges of regret for turning down James Donovan's dinner invitation. There were worse ways to spend an evening than eating on an expense account with an attractive man and his sexy accent. But she knew a womanizer when she saw one, and Mr. Donovan was much too irresistible to get tangled up with, even for a few days.

She pulled on a faded Grateful Dead T-shirt that barely covered her cotton undies and released her dark shoulder-length hair from its chignon, frowning when she remembered *his* comment about her hairstyle. But she smirked when she surveyed her legs, still and always her best physical attribute. After further, more critical perusal in the full-length mirror, Kat sprawled on the wood floor in her bedroom and performed one hundred sit-ups.

Out of breath, she dug her ratty, pink, fuzzy house shoes from the bottom of her closet and hopped to the living room as she put them on. After phoning in the pizza order, she picked up the thriller she'd half read. At exactly seven, the doorbell rang, and Kat rose from the couch, still reading the book she carried.

She absently unlocked the two deadbolts on the door, then swung it open to greet her friend.

James Donovan stood in the doorway, dressed in casual attire and unabashedly studying her legs.

Kat's tongue felt wooden, her limbs paralyzed.

He glanced up and grinned lazily. "Hallo, Pussy-Kat."

TWO

James knew he would forever remember the look on Katherine McKray's face as she stood in the doorway of her flat. Her fetching mouth was relaxed in a most becoming way, and behind those schoolmarm's glasses, the dark blue irises of her eyes were generously framed in white. "You're a truthful woman, Ms. McKray, your legs are indeed beautiful."

Her mouth snapped shut and she drew back her shoulders, inadvertently exposing a few more inches of thigh for his enjoyment. "How did you know where I live?"

He smiled. "I can assure you I've tackled more challenging tasks in my career."

"You've got ten seconds to explain why you're here."

"You're not wearing a watch."

"One Mississippi, two Mississippi—"

"It's simple." James shrugged. "I was hoping to persuade you to change your mind about sharing a meal." He reached forward and plucked the novel from her hand. After studying its cover, he made a clicking sound with his cheek. "You prefer a paperback to my company? I'm wounded, Ms. McKray."

Kat snatched the book out of his hand. "For your information, Mr. Donovan—"

"Please call me James, all my friends do."

Her eyes blazed. "For your information, *Mr. Donovan*, I'm expecting company."

He studied her carefully, inch by inch, from the top of her mussed hair to the curled toes of her horrid slippers. "And this is someone you wish to impress?"

"Good night, Mr. Donovan." She slammed the door in his face.

The sound vibrated throughout the worn hallway, followed by the purposeful thwack, thwack, of both deadbolts turning. He shifted from foot to foot, waiting for inspiration to strike him. Damn, she was a spirited woman!

"Hello," came a voice down the hall.

He turned to see a skinny redhead with a duffel bag slung over her shoulder approaching him warily.

"Are you here to see Kat?" she asked, her head angled skeptically.

"Yes," he said quickly. "I was just about to knock." He gave her his most charming grin. "The name is James Donovan." She stuck a limp hand into the one he extended.

"Denise Womack," she said brightly, dropping her guard.

Gesturing to the door, he said, "I wasn't sure this was the right place. I met Kat at the museum today."

"You're British, aren't you?" she asked, as if he were a rare specimen.

He bit back a smile. "I suppose my accent would make it difficult to convince you otherwise."

Her eyes widened. "Oh! Are you connected with the king's letter?"

"Indirectly."

"Is that why you're here?"

"Actually I came to see if Ms. McKray would join me for supper."

The woman grinned. "Really?"

A true-blue, matchmaking friend, he noted with delight. Conjuring up a worried frown, he said, "I hope I'm not imposing on plans the two of you made."

"Heavens, no," she said with a wave. "Kat was only going to watch me do laundry."

"Ah, splendid," he said, reaching for her laundry bag. "I'll let you knock since it's you she's expecting."

"Sure," she said agreeably, then pounded on the door.

After a pause, he heard a slight movement inside the apartment. "Who is it?" Kat demanded.

"It's me, Kat," Denise said, winking at James conspiratorially. He winked back.

Kat opened the door, and Denise chirped, "Look who I found in the hall."

"Hallo, Pussy-Kat," he said cheerfully.

Kat stared at James with pursed lips. "Don't call me that. And why are you still here?"

Denise frowned. "Kat, Mr. Donovan wants to take you to dinner." She leaned forward and added through clenched teeth, "And I assured him you are *not* busy tonight."

"But I've already ordered the pizza."

Her friend glared. "I can eat the whole thing by myself anyway."

"Liar," Kat said, then held up her novel. "And I was just getting to the good part."

Denise scoffed. "The college professor did it because the guy was boinking his wife."

Kat's mouth dropped open, and she stamped her foot. "I can't *believe* you told me the end of the story! You *know* I hate that!"

Denise grabbed the book and tossed it into a nearby chair. "Go out and have some fun!"

Hands on hips, Kat glared past her friend to focus on him.

He smiled innocently and shrugged. "Can you blame me for wanting to dine with a beautiful woman instead of all by myself?"

Her friend moaned. "Kat," she hissed out the side of her mouth, "if you don't go with him, I *will.*"

Kat rolled her eyes. He laughed and deposited the bag of laundry inside the door. "We'll go somewhere nearby, Ms. McKray—anywhere you like."

She was nibbling on that delicious looking lower lip, wavering.

"I'll have you back in an hour," he added, crossing his heart with his index finger.

Denise grabbed his arm and pulled him inside, then kicked the door shut. "Have a seat and give her ten minutes," she said, then turned a protesting Kat around and herded her toward the bedroom.

After the door closed with a resounding boom, James stood and looked around Ms. Katherine McKray's flat, hoping to glean something about this fiery woman's background. He was surprised at the character of the rooms: the rich wood floors, the ornate mantels of two corner fireplaces, the floor-to-ceiling bookshelves. Her furniture was an eclectic collection of denim-covered loveseats, velvet footstools, and impressionist-colored cushions. As he would have expected, tasteful and interesting artwork dotted the walls, the tables, and even the floor in the form of hand-painted rugs.

He stepped closer to her bookshelves to scan the titles there. Lots of art history books, and several museum catalogs. A few movies: *Gone With the Wind, Casablanca,* and *An Affair to Remember.* He grinned. Pussy-Kat was a bit sappy, it seemed.

Out of all the bric-a-brac lining the bookshelves, only two framed photos were displayed. One older photo of a youngish couple, presumably her parents, judging from the woman's resemblance to Kat. And a recent one of Kat and a middle-aged man, whom he determined to also be her father. James frowned. Her mother must have died or left the family some years ago.

Through swinging doors to the right, he could see a neat white kitchenette with bright Mexican tile accents. To the left, a tiny hallway that led to an outside balcony with no view apparently doubled as her work area. A shelf of various refinishing solvents testified to a serious hobby. A set of tall wood shutters were being stripped of several layers of paint. The woman obviously didn't mind getting her hands dirty.

When he turned back to the sitting room, an object in the corner caught his eye and he stepped over to inspect it more closely. Thoroughly impressed, he caressed the knobby surface of a brass-inlaid mahogany humidor the size of a breadbox, then carefully turned the tiny tasseled key and lifted the lid. "Bloody hell," he breathed as the rich scent of fresh tobacco filled his nostrils. He lifted one of the cigars lovingly.

"They're Cuban," came Kat's voice from the other side of the room.

James turned to find her leaning against the wall, arms crossed over a demure white cardigan sweater atop wide-leg black pants. Her rich dark hair had been twisted into a somewhat looser knot—Denise's touch, he presumed. She was not smiling.

"I know," he said, looking back to the cigar he held. "Hoyo De Monterrey Double Coronas—the best." And according to the long-running U.S. Cuban embargo, quite illegal, he noted. "Are these yours?"

"They were my father's," she said, pushing away from the wall and walking toward him slowly.

"Were?"

"He died last year. I saved his cigars—the smell reminds me of him."

Her voice sounded steady, but the total lack of emotion betrayed the effort she expended to sound casual. He could tell she'd been devastated by her father's death, and he felt a pang of sympathy. Although relatively sure she juniored his thirty-seven years only by a half dozen or so, at this moment she looked as vulnerable as a child.

"You've taken exceptional care of them." He replaced the cigar carefully among the two dozen or so identical ones remaining, then lowered the lid.

"Replenishing the water in his humidor is a small thing to do to preserve something he loved," she said softly.

"I'm sure he would be pleased," James said, stifling the urge to fold her into his arms. He shook himself mentally. Lust was a comfortable, familiar emotion—sometimes he conquered it, sometimes he surrendered to it. But this sudden . . . affection . . . was unsettling. "Are you ready?"

She lifted one eyebrow. "Are you through snooping?"

He grinned sheepishly. "Forgive me, I was quite intrigued."

She simply inclined her head, and James felt as if they'd reached some kind of understanding.

"Where's your friend?" he asked.

"She's using the phone in my room—I guess it's her way of giving us some privacy."

"I'm indebted to her for her efforts."

"Don't feel so special," she warned. "This week alone she tried to set me up with the pest control sprayer, the meter reader, and the guy who delivers for the Chinese restaurant down the street."

Holding the door open, James acknowledged her outfit with a wry smile. "Very nice, but do you always dress so, um, warmly?"

Kat was donning a long all-weather coat, but stopped mid-motion, tossed it on a chair, and stuck her tongue out at him. He rather liked it. Stepping into the hall, he asked, "Where are we going?"

"To Torbett's, about six blocks over. The food is good, the utensils are clean, and there's usually a little jazz band playing."

"Hmmm, sounds romantic," he murmured, draping an arm around her waist.

She stopped and carefully removed his hand, then continued walking out of the building.

It was a balmy August evening, but a salty wind from the bay nipped at his cheeks. Suddenly, James understood Kat's penchant for sweaters.

"The rains will begin soon," she said morosely.

"I'm sure it's good for attendance at the museum," he said with a smile.

"That's true," she said, smiling back.

She had a very pretty face, he decided. Not model perfect, but striking, to be sure. Animated and fresh, Kat looked vibrant and interesting, and James found himself already planning ways to extend their time past the hour he'd promised her. He could always catch a flight to New York tomorrow.

After they descended the stairs to the sidewalk, she asked, "Shall we walk or take a taxi?"

"Neither," he said, pointing. "I was able to rent a passable car for the duration of my short stay."

Kat followed his finger and blinked. "The black Jaguar?"

Nodding, he said, "It'll do in a pinch."

Okay, Kat acknowledged begrudgingly, not only did the man have good taste in clothes and cigars, but he scored high in the automobile category, too. James unlocked the door with a keyless remote and held open the passenger door for her. "Remind me never to show you the heap I drive," she said as she lowered herself into the squeaky leather seat.

Panic rose in her throat after he slid into his seat and the slight vacuum seal of the door isolated them in the intimate interior of the car. Everything about this man screamed danger to her emotional well-being. Not that her instincts had always led her down the right road, she admitted ruefully.

She glanced at him out of the corner of her eye. His dark hair was slicked back and he smelled faintly of strong soap. He'd traded his Italian suit for dark brown slacks, a thin long-sleeved jersey, and a tan leather vest. Kat winced. Denise was right, the man was gorgeous.

When he shifted gears, she saw a flash of metal at his waist. Incredulous, she asked, "Are you carrying a gun to dinner?"

His smile was tight-lipped. "Madam, I carry a gun to the *shower*."

Kat perused his profile carefully. She didn't really know this man at all. "Am I in danger?"

His dimple made an appearance. "Most definitely," he said huskily, then settled his dark gaze on her. "And I feel obligated to tell you I have more than one weapon on my person."

Kat jerked her head back to look at the street in front of them and swallowed hard.

Torbett's was crowded, but most patrons were hanging around the bar listening to the live music. They only had to wait a few minutes before their names were called. James stubbornly kept his hand on her waist as they wound their way to a small table in a corner beneath a hanging stained-glass lamp. She felt the imprint of his warm fingers even after she slid into the seat he pulled out for her.

"Would you share a bottle of wine with me?" he asked Kat when the waitress arrived.

She nodded, giving in to the shiver of desire that raced up her spine at the sound of his voice. And she wasn't the only woman affected, she noticed wryly. The waitress had nearly swooned when James spoke. When he bestowed the woman with a killer smile, Kat pressed her lips together and shook her head. Pity to the woman who lost her heart to this man. Because she'd spend the rest of her life sharing him with every female who crossed his path.

"Very good choice," he said, looking around and nodding with approval.

She smiled, her heart sinking with the realization that even the table between them could not keep him from crowding her senses. Feeling woefully out of control, Kat willed her pulse to slow as she methodically studied the menu for something low-calorie.

"What do you recommend?" he asked, flicking his gaze toward her over the menu.

"If you like seafood, the grouper is wonderful, otherwise the rib-eye steak is the house specialty."

"What are you having?"

The white lasagna spoke to her, but she laid the menu aside. "Probably a salad."

He frowned. "Are you one of those rabbit eaters?"

She gave him a wry grin. "Do I look like one of those rabbit eaters?"

James leaned to the side and slowly let his eyes sweep her figure head to toe. "I quite like the way you look. Your friend is frightfully skinny."

"Denise is a runway model," Kat explained. "She looks great in designer clothes."

He lifted one eyebrow. "I can assure you, Pussy-Kat, men are much more concerned about how a woman looks *out* of her clothes."

Kat's breasts tightened, and—thankfully—at that moment, the waitress brought their wine. James nodded, then waved the woman away, preferring to pour it himself. Watching the pale liquid splash into her glass, Kat felt herself relax slightly. Sure, the man was a little arrogant, but it felt good to be in the company of someone who was comfortable with himself. And with whom she felt so comfortable. . . .

His eyes danced as he raised his glass to hers. "To the beginning of a beautiful friendship."

Lifting the glass to her lips, she said, "I have the feeling you've made that toast hundreds of times."

He pulled a wounded face. "Pussy-Kat, give me more credit . . . I've made that toast *thousands* of times."

She shook her head and laughed. "Is that your fail-proof line for getting lucky?"

"Do you think I'm trying to get lucky?"

Kat set down her glass. "Yes."

He flashed even, white teeth. "Good. And what are my chances at this point?"

Glancing down to study the hem of the napkin, Kat wet her lips carefully. The man was outrageously appealing, but she didn't engage in casual sex. Besides, something about James Donovan made her feel very vulnerable, dredging up the old nightmares of stepping onto the stage of a packed stadium and suddenly realizing you were stark naked. She lifted her gaze to his expectant one, and shook her head slightly. "I'm not the girl for you, James. If you want entertainment, it's still early and I'm sure you could—"

"Yes," he cut in, "I'm sure I could." He gave her a small smile, then reached over to cover her hand with his. "But I assure you, Kat, I'm exactly where I want to be." His smile widened, giving her a brief glimpse of his elusive dimples. "Especially since it appears we have progressed to a first-name basis."

His mood was infectious, and she smiled, ignoring the rush of desire triggered by the brief touch of his hand. The waitress returned and Kat ordered lasagna, James, the steak.

"Tell me about yourself," he said when they were alone again.

Kat shrugged. "You already know what I do for a living, and where I live."

"What about family?"

"There's just me," she said brightly. "My mother died when I was a teenager, and you know about my father. Actually, it was my father who introduced me to the museum. He worked at Jellico's for over fifteen years."

"A family affair, eh?"

Kat squashed the troubling memories that threatened to surface. "You might say that."

"You don't seem to get along with your boss—Mr. Trent, isn't it?"

Deciding it was useless to lie, Kat nodded. "We don't always see eye to eye. Guy has grown increasingly more commercial in his pursuits for the museum."

"The owner must favor him."

Kat rolled her eyes. "The owner is his brother-in-law and lives in San Diego, so Guy has the run of the place."

"Ah. And how do you feel about showing King George's letter?"

"Fine," she said. "Once I know it's authentic. What can you tell me about Lady Mercer?" Seeing the look that crossed his face, Kat quickly clarified her statement. "Skip the sordid details."

His mouth twisted as he thought. "Tania Mercer is a widow and a shrewd businesswoman. Her elderly husband left her a tidy sum, but she's grown it considerably since his death."

"Is she a patron of the arts?"

"Yes," he said slowly. "If it suits her purposes. She dabbles in the stock market and start-up ventures, too. She also has a keen interest in rare antiques—I suppose it would follow that she would jump at a chance to purchase the letter in hopes of attaining a handsome profit."

"So you believe she came by the letter honestly?"

He frowned slightly, then said, "I've never known of Tania doing anything fraudulent—underhanded, perhaps, but not blatantly illegal."

She nodded, satisfied. "What about you, James?" she asked. "Do you have a family?"

"A sister in London," he said, a look of genuine affection crossing his face. "You rather remind me of her, actually."

Kat bit back a frown—she wasn't ready to jump into bed with the man, but being compared to his sister wasn't top of her list either. "Are the two of you close?"

Nodding, he said, "We don't visit as often as we should, but she's a terrific girl, and married to a good fellow. Expecting a baby in the spring."

"And you're retired?"

"Yes."

"So you spend your time jetting across the world doing favors for old lovers?"

He smiled. "It passes the time."

"You sound bored."

"It's a bit of a change, going from a very active job to playing chess and puttering in the garden."

"Somehow, I can't see you weeding begonias."

"I enjoy the quieter aspects of life, and I'm still a consultant for the agency, but I confess I miss the assignments."

Kat finished her wine and held her glass as he refilled it. "So why did you retire?"

"Twenty years seemed long enough—I was still a lad when I was recruited. And I have all the money I'll ever need."

She straightened and pushed her glasses higher on her nose. Was he bragging, or just stating a fact?

Their entrées arrived, and James declared her recommendation an excellent choice. The music grew louder as the meal progressed, so they stopped talking and enjoyed the sounds and tastes, communicating with gestures and glances, and emptying the bottle of wine. Kat couldn't remember when she'd had a more delightful evening. Over coffee, the thought flitted across her mind that his company *was* rather pleasant, and she was suddenly disappointed that he would be leaving so soon.

He paid the tab, then walked close to her as they returned to the car. On the short drive home, he asked questions about the city, and Kat, a Bay Area native, gave him an abbreviated history.

It seemed all too soon that he was walking her to her door, and Kat's pulse was racing.

"I've kept you longer than the hour I promised," he said near her ear as she unlocked the door.

She laughed nervously. "I noticed. You'll be running through the airport, but you should still make your flight." At last the door swung open before her, and she turned, smiling brightly. "Thank you for dinner." She stuck out her hand.

He studied her hand for a few seconds, then frowned. "No good-night kiss, Pussy-Kat?"

"That's not necessary," she said quickly.

His smile was slow and nerve-racking. "Speak for yourself," he said, then pulled her to him and lowered his mouth to hers, his tongue urging her to open to him. Kat did, allowing him a deep, slow exploration. Her mind spun and her knees weakened as his tongue conquered hers. He held her body tightly against his, and she tentatively fingered the wall of muscle across his back. When she felt his obvious arousal against her stomach, she stiffened.

James lifted his head and slowly released her. "I apologize, Pussy-Kat. I lost my head," he said, then cleared his throat. He gave her a proper smile, then nodded curtly. "Thank you for a lovely evening. I sincerely hope our paths cross again sometime."

Still stunned at the desire flooding her limbs, Kat could only blink and right her glasses in response. When he strode down the hall and disappeared around the corner, she touched her swollen lips and expelled a breath she hadn't realized she'd been holding.

Turning, Kat stumbled into her apartment and closed the door. Under a lone glowing lamp, Denise had left a note to call tomorrow with all the details. Kat sighed and walked into her bedroom, then sank onto the bed in darkness. The clock glowed ten twenty-five. Hesitant to part with the heady feeling of James's electric kiss, she lay back on her bed, fully clothed, and closed her eyes to troubled dreams of a cigar-smoking, smooth-talking foreigner.

The peal of the phone startled her from a deep sleep. Kat sat up and swung her legs over the side of the bed, feeling for her glasses on the nightstand. "Who in the world would be calling at two in the morning?" she croaked into the darkness. She grabbed the handset. "Hello?"

"Kat, this is James Donovan." His voice sounded grave. "I skipped the flight, then I couldn't sleep, so I drove by the gallery. You'd better get down here."

Suddenly she was fully awake. "What's wrong?"

"From what I can see, three unconscious guards, and if my instincts are correct, one missing letter."

THREE

James scanned the motley crew assembled before him in the brightly lit hallway of the museum. Guy Trent was extremely agitated, running his fingers through his sparse hair. Six security guards, including the two men and one woman who had been asleep when he arrived, were talking and gesturing among themselves. Two police officers were gazing at the high ceiling as if the perpetrator might still be lurking up there somewhere. And the fat detective who had just arrived was snapping a wad of gum in a most irritating manner.

He had just shaken hands with the snappy Detective Tenner when a buzz sounded and Kat emerged through a rear door, then jogged down the hall toward the group. A long, grubby white cardigan flapped around her. She was still dressed in her dinner clothes, slightly worse for wear, but she'd taken time to yank her hair back into an eyestretching ponytail.

"What happened?" she asked breathlessly as she came to a stop before him.

James introduced her to the detective and the policemen, then started at the beginning. "When I drove by around one-thirty this morning, I noticed a flashing light inside, but I couldn't rouse a response from security. A few minutes later, two relief guards came on duty and we discovered their three comrades unconscious at their posts."

He motioned toward the group of guards, who quieted instantly at his gesture.

"Carl, what happened?" Kat asked the groggy looking veteran.

The guy shrugged. "Don't know—something made us all fall asleep."

A police officer cut in, holding up a foam cup. "We've taken a sample to be sure, but we think someone may have drugged the coffee."

Kat's boss shifted uncomfortably, his bald head shiny with sweat. "The Maya display is intact, as well as the Navajo exhibit. The Twila paintings are still in the vault, thank God. If anything besides the king's letter is missing, it's small."

"It could have been much worse," Kat said, puffing out her cheeks in a relieved exhale.

"I doubt Lady Mercer will agree," James felt obliged to say, faintly chafed that Kat seemed unconcerned.

She threw him an impatient frown.

Guy's uneasiness seemed to be growing. Detective Tenner turned to Kat's boss. "So we're dealing with a premeditated crime—and the thief had a specific goal. What's the letter worth?"

Guy worked his mouth as he pondered the question. "It has yet to be authenticated, so right now, on the black market to a serious collector—maybe twenty thousand."

"Is it insured?" the detective pressed.

Guy deferred to Kat with a glance and she nodded. "By a European fine arts insurer. I think I remember seeing the figure of twenty-five thousand on the paperwork."

Tenner popped his gum. "And what would it go for if it's real?"

Guy shrugged. "It depends—interest in the letter is running high right now—I know the Handelman family is prepared to pay two hundred fifty thousand. In a heated auction, it could bring five hundred thousand or more."

The detective nodded. Pop, pop went the gum. "Okay, so how did the thief get inside the vault?"

"No sign of forced entry," a tall, trim guard said quickly. "They had to have a badge for one of the museum entrances and also for the vault."

Eyebrows raised, Tenner asked, "And you are?"

"Ronald Beaman," the man answered. "Head of security here at the museum."

"And how many staff members have access to the vault?"

"Only a handful of senior staff members—maybe five or six, including Ms. McKray and Mr. Trent. We can check the electronic log to see whose badge was used." He motioned to two of the guards and they disappeared quickly.

"I'll need fingerprints lifted inside the vault," Detective Tenner piped in.

"Which should corroborate the film," James said, pointing to a camera mounted high on the wall.

Beaman winced. "Well, not necessarily. We've been having trouble lately with the cameras, but if we're lucky, maybe we caught something." James resisted the urge to roll his eyes and joined the others as they followed the security officer through a maze of hallways and small rooms to a security console.

It took Guy and Ronald Beaman several minutes to find the correct camera monitor and rewind the tape. While they were waiting, Andy Wharton arrived. With his hair loose around his shoulders and looking none too tidy, he'd clearly just rolled out of bed.

"Is everyone all right?" he gasped.

Guy nodded quickly, then waved impatiently toward the monitor.

Everyone crowded in for a look, and James made room for Kat in front of him, enjoying the slight brush of their bodies. But she was completely absorbed in the video, trying to hide the nervous shaking of her hands.

Ron Beaman fast-forwarded the gritty, static-plagued film at a moderate speed until they saw a figure appear, then he pushed the play button, and everyone leaned closer. James's eyes immediately darted to the time on the film. Twelve thirty-seven A.M.

They watched as the person walked up the hall in semidarkness, becoming larger and a bit clearer as the distance to the camera closed. It appeared to be a woman. James frowned, thinking something about the person seemed familiar to him, then his breath froze at the same time he felt Kat's body stiffen.

The person's face was hidden by a large, floppy hat, but dark, shoulder-length hair swept over the collar of a belted all-weather coat, identical to the one he'd seen tossed onto a chair earlier this evening. Gloves covered the woman's hands, and she was wearing a skirt that hung lower than the coat, but not long enough to cover slender ankles and clunky high-heeled shoes—just like the ones Kat had been wearing yesterday. The woman

badged into the vault room with the confidence of someone familiar with the procedure.

"Kat?" Andy whispered, lowering horn-rimmed
glasses for a better look at the screen.

"Kat?" Guy sputtered incredulously. "You were in
the vault after midnight?"

"No!" she gasped, concern in her voice. "That's not
me."

They continued to watch the distorted tape in palpa-
ble silence, and within a few seconds the figure emerged
from the vault with the environmentally controlled box
beneath her arm. And even though the woman's face was
still shrouded, James caught the glimpse of something
shiny beneath the hat as the figure turned. Spectacles?
His eyes darted to Kat's wire-rimmed glasses just as she
pushed them higher on her nose.

Guy turned to Kat. "What the hell is going on
here?"

James studied her reactions carefully. Kat was still
staring at the video, watching the figure retreat down the
hall and disappear off camera. "I have no idea, but that is
not me."

At that moment, two security guards rejoined them.
"Here's the log, Mr. Trent." Guy snatched it from their
hands and ran his finger down the computer printout.
He scowled, then pursed his lips. He raised his gaze long
enough to glare at Kat, then read, "Enter rear staff entrance, badge number one three five, Katherine McKray,
twelve thirty-five A.M. Enter painting vault, badge number one three five, Katherine McKray, twelve thirty-
seven A.M." His voice escalated. "Exit painting vault,
badge number one three five, Katherine McKray, twelve
thirty-nine A.M. Exit rear staff entrance, badge number
one three five, Katherine McKray, twelve-forty A.M."

All eyes were on Kat, who was slowly shaking her head. Andy Wharton stared at her, openmouthed. The two police officers edged closer.

"Let me see that!" she demanded, grabbing the log. She scanned the sheet, and tossed it on a table. "That's impossible—I wasn't here!"

Detective Tenner turned toward her. "Then you have an airtight alibi from twelve to one o'clock this morning?"

James's heart sank at the guilty look on her face. "I-I was asleep," she stuttered.

Tenner picked at his teeth. "Alone?"

"Yes," she said through clenched teeth.

"I see," Detective Tenner said. "In that case, we're going to need you to come down to the station for questioning."

"This is crazy!" she ranted, her eyes swinging to James. "I didn't steal the letter! I wasn't here, I tell you."

Hiding his alarm, James put a calming hand on her arm. "Relax, Kat." He turned to the detective with an ingratiating smile. "Sir, don't you think it odd that the lady would allow herself to be captured on tape?"

"I told Ms. McKray just yesterday that the cameras were on the blink," Ronald Beaman offered quietly.

James's heart thudded as his gaze swung back to Kat. Pale and sweaty, hers was not the face of a woman who had nothing to hide. Had she actually burglarized her own gallery? "Detective, can't you take her statement here?"

Tenner's laugh was dry. "Not if she's the thief, Mr. Donovan. I don't know how you do it in England, but here we make an arrest if we have a video of the person carrying off the goods."

"This is ridiculous!" Kat exclaimed, spreading her

arms wide. She turned to her boss. "Come on, Guy, we've had our differences, but you know I'd never do something like this."

Guy looked her up and down with contempt. "All I have to say, Katherine McKray, is 'like father, like daughter.' "

She blanched and James wondered what the man was referring to. She'd mentioned her father had worked for the museum—had he been connected to some wrongdoing?

James stepped in and raised his hands. "Before we clamp on the handcuffs, gentlemen, let's consider another possibility."

Guy Trent crossed his arms. "Which is?"

"Perhaps someone dressed up as Ms. McKray to pull off the heist." He turned to Kat. "Where do you keep your security badge?"

"Hidden in my bedroom," she said slowly.

"Do you remember putting your badge in its usual place last night when you arrived home from work?"

"Wait a minute," Detective Tenner said, waving his arms. "I'm supposed to be asking the questions here."

James frowned. "Sorry—you may proceed."

Tenner harrumphed, turned to Kat and pulled out a small pad of paper, then clicked a cheap ballpoint pen, poised to write. "Now then, do you remember putting your badge in its usual place last night when you arrived home from work?"

She bit on her lower lip. "I-I think so—yes, but I left so quickly when James called a few minutes ago, I didn't even think to bring it with me."

"Kat," James said calmly, "was anything disturbed in your apartment last night when you went inside?"

Her eyes widened. "I didn't turn on any lights—I went straight to bed."

"What time was that?" Tenner asked.

Kat and James answered at the same time. "Around ten-thirty."

The detective's eyebrows shot up. "You were with her, Mr. Donovan?"

James bristled at the man's accusatory glance. "We had dinner and I walked her to her door."

"Was anyone else in your apartment last night?" the man pressed. "Or more specifically, your bedroom?"

Kat looked cross. "No! Wait—there's my friend Denise. She was at my apartment doing her laundry when I left with James—er, Mr. Donovan."

"Short hair or long?" Tenner asked.

"Short and red," Kat said. "But Denise doesn't have anything to do with this."

"We'll be the judge of that," the detective said, then wrote down Denise's name and address. "What about the getup the thief was wearing?" he asked Kat. "If we searched your apartment, Ms. McKray, would we find a hat and coat?"

Kat glanced at James, worry in her eyes, then looked back to Tenner. "Yes, I have a coat like that, and lots of hats, but so does nearly every woman in this city."

"And," James noted, "if someone stole Ms. McKray's badge, it would have been quite simple to steal a few articles of her clothing as well."

Tenner looked unconvinced. "And grow hair, too, I suppose?"

"They could have worn a wig," James pointed out.

The detective sighed dramatically. "Ms. McKray, give me one good reason why I shouldn't place you under arrest right now."

"Because," she said, crossing her arms, "I didn't do it."

Tenner pursed his lips and nodded. "Okay, let's see if I've got this straight: We need to be on the lookout for someone who looks like you, dresses like you, has knowledge of this letter, and has the same access to the museum." He popped his gum. "Do I look like a fool, Ms. McKray?"

James bit his tongue to keep from answering for her.

Kat rolled her eyes. "Do I look like a thief, Mr. Tenner?"

"I just call it like I see it, ma'am." He nodded to one of the policemen. "Read her her rights."

Kat looked at James, fear brimming in her blue eyes.

James gave her a reassuring smile. "Don't worry, Pussy-Kat, everything will be all right."

But worry boiled in his stomach. Either Kat McKray was a very good actress, or someone was out to frame her. Regardless, the fetching woman was in a great deal of trouble.

FOUR

James fisted his hands at his sides as the younger policeman, Officer Raines, withdrew handcuffs. The man's
partner and senior by at least two decades, Officer
Campbell, began reciting the Miranda warnings in a
practiced tone. Kat's blue eyes widened as she heard the
charges of unlawful entry and burglary. She backed up a
step, touching her hand to her temple, slowly shaking
her head in denial.

"Detective Tenner," James said, trying to keep his
voice calm for her sake, "is it really necessary to subdue
the lady?" He smirked. "I'm sure your two able officers
can tackle her if she attempts to escape."

"Just following procedure, Mr. Donovan," the detective assured him. "She's under arrest."

A din erupted in the room. Guy and Andy stepped
back to the perimeter, as if Kat were suddenly a dangerous quantity. The security guards talked quietly among
themselves.

"Wait!" Kat said, holding up her hands.

Everyone stilled. James had the horrible feeling she

was about to admit her wrongdoing. Her mouth trembled. "G-Give me a minute with Mr. Donovan, please, Detective Tenner."

Quelling a bolt of surprise, James hid his apprehension beneath a weak smirk.

Tenner squinted at her, then nodded curtly. James moved to her side and she grasped his arm as if he were a lifeline, then pulled him out of earshot of the others. "James," she whispered urgently, "here is a key to my apartment." He felt the metal pressing into his forearm beneath her splayed hand. "Please go immediately and remove my father's humidor. The police will confiscate it for sure if they find his cigars." She choked on the last word, her eyes brimming with tears.

Incredulity washed over him. She was about to be hauled off to jail for a serious crime, and she was worried about her father's cigars. He searched the depths of her watery blue eyes and didn't like what he saw: guilt, sadness, desperation. He lifted his hand slowly and, ever so gently, tipped her chin up with his forefinger. "No confession, Pussy-Kat?" he asked softly.

He felt her throat constrict beneath his finger as she swallowed, but her gaze never left his. Footsteps approached them from behind. "Promise me you'll get the cigars," she whispered fiercely, a single tear spilling down her pale cheek.

And without warning, something strange and a bit frightening wrapped itself around his heart and cinched itself tight. He admired loyalty above all things. He studied the contours of her lovely, troubled face. Although he'd always harbored a soft spot for curvy, smoldering brunettes, he'd never been so compelled to invest himself in a woman's cause, and certainly not after extracting a solitary, reluctant kiss.

"James?" she murmured.

He didn't speak, but simply jerked his chin down in acquiescence and captured the key beneath his own hand just as the police officer swinging the cuffs walked up.

"It's time, Ms. McKray," Detective Tenner said loudly from across the room.

Kat swung her head around and stared blankly at Tenner and Officer Raines, offering no resistance as the young man smiled sadly and gently clasped her hands behind her. She did, however, blink as the handcuffs clinked into place.

"Kat," Andy said, as she was led past him, "is there someone I can call?" His words were kind enough, but he sent worried glances toward his glaring boss.

Her eyes darted in scattered thought, then she nodded and said over her shoulder. "Valmer Getty."

James turned to follow the policemen and Kat to the parking lot, but Detective Tenner called after him when he had almost made it out the door. "We're not finished with you, Mr. Donovan."

James pasted on an amiable smile and, still walking, turned back to the man with a small salute. "I'll be back, Detective. Just want to make sure the lady gets to the station in one piece."

Tenner raised an eyebrow suggestively.

James attempted to snuff the man's suspicion with a stern look. "After allowing the letter to be stolen, it's the least I owe my client, Lady Mercer," he said, exiting before Tenner could respond.

Outside, he glanced around the parking lot, somehow knowing the beat-up Volkswagen van was Kat's the instant he spotted it. After climbing into his rented car, he watched in uncomfortable silence as the officers assisted Kat into the squad car, its lights flashing silently in the pre-dawn hour. Kat turned and looked at him as the car pulled away, her eyes reminding him of his promise. He made as if to follow the police car, then purposely slowed at a stoplight and lost them, heading instead toward her apartment.

Kat watched him disappear from view in the side mirror and exhaled a pent-up breath. She shifted sideways to alleviate the immediate discomfort of having her hands cuffed behind her, but nothing could dispel the sickening swell of panic in her stomach. Her heart pounded erratically. She sank against the cold seat and closed her eyes, fighting the dizziness that threatened to overwhelm her. *I will not pass out . . . I will not pass out. . . .*

She opened her eyes to try to focus on something, but the sight of the wall of crisscrossed metal between her and the officers talking quietly in the front seat triggered another wave of nausea. Kat gagged, then leaned forward and vomited on the floor. The sudden braking of the car nearly tumbled her, but she caught herself with a jarring blow to her shoulder as Officer Campbell pulled into a convenience store parking lot.

"You should have told us you were feeling sick," Officer Raines chided gently as he helped her from the backseat and unlocked her cuffs. The other policeman handed her a wad of tissues, which she gratefully accepted to wipe her mouth.

The men appeared to be at a loss for a few seconds, then the older officer mumbled something about getting it cleaned up and walked toward the store.

"Don't worry," Officer Raines said kindly. "I've seen much worse."

"I didn't steal that letter."

The young man shifted uncomfortably, obviously unconvinced. "Your lawyer will be able to help you."

Kat's spirits lifted a fraction as the image of Valmer Getty, her father's friend and attorney, came to her. She yearned for one of Val's bear hugs. He'd convince the police and the district attorney that the charges against her were ridiculous. She watched Officer Campbell pour a box of baking soda over the mess she'd made and wished all her problems could be so easily absorbed. To her relief, Campbell waved off the cuffs when Raines reluctantly withdrew them again. They shepherded her into the backseat and were soon under way again.

"Looks like we lost your friend," Campbell noted with a glance in the rearview mirror.

Kat nodded, trying to look miserable, then realized it wasn't really a stretch for her at this moment. A strange feeling uncoiled in her chest when she thought of James Donovan. He was a virtual stranger and represented the owner of the document she had been accused of stealing, yet he was the person in the room to whom she'd turned for help. Even if he didn't believe in her innocence, she felt certain he would do as he'd promised.

The memory of his lips and body pressed against hers seemed especially powerful now, when she felt so alone. She'd been seriously involved with a handful of men in her thirty-one years, but not one of their lovemaking sessions had left her feeling as desirable as James's lone kiss. Without thinking, she brought her shaking fingers to her mouth and brushed them across her bare lips. Then she shook herself, astonished that her mind could be elsewhere in her predicament.

Under arrest and on her way to the hoosegow, very probably out of a job and, at the very least, bearing a tarnished reputation—and she was daydreaming about a smooth talker who probably collected American women like souvenir figurines.

She was in big trouble—literally and emotionally— and intuition told her the situation would worsen before it improved. The clawing panic she'd felt earlier settled into a cold stone of terror in the pit of her stomach. For the first time since her father's death, she was glad he wasn't around to see her. Or to be mired in yet another scandal surrounding his beloved gallery.

Before inserting the key Kat had given him, James inspected the series of deadbolts for signs of tampering, but found none. If someone had entered her apartment, it was with a key or through another entrance, unless her friend Denise had left it unlocked.

Wearing latex gloves, James opened the door and eased into her flat. In one glance he noticed the long coat was not where she had tossed it the previous evening, but other than the cushions on her couch being in slight disarray, nothing else seemed amiss. He noted the humidor in the corner, then headed toward her bedroom. The police probably wouldn't arrive for a couple of hours, but he didn't wish to arouse suspicion with his unexplained absence. Besides, he wanted to help guide the questioning of the others at the gallery. Since Tenner was already convinced of Kat's guilt, James suspected the detective would be woefully inept.

Her bedroom looked comfortably equipped with a large bed and simple, eclectic furnishings. The walls were textured white on white, sparsely adorned with simple framed posters. The pale linens were gender neutral, absent of ruffles and floral prints. The impression of her body was clear in the rumpled comforter.

James wasn't in such a hurry that he didn't spend a few seconds imagining her lying there sprawled on the covers, her dark hair loose and trailing over the edge of the bed. The woman really was quite delectable, even though she seemed to attract trouble—which, on second thought, could be an exciting quality.

His mouth worked as he pondered the state of the room. She hadn't even bothered to turn down the spread . . . as if she were only going to be there for a short time. James pulled at his chin. Had she just returned from burglarizing the gallery? She hadn't exactly denied it when he had pressed her. In fact, he would have bet his gold watch that she was hiding something. But none of it smacked of the Kat he'd become acquainted with the night before.

Still, he professionally canvassed the room for likely hiding places for either the letter or the case it had been stored in. Nothing. He found her security badge in the bottom of a jewelry box, but didn't touch it. Next he opened the folding doors to her closet and blinked at the multitude of colored boxes stacked knee-high. Pussy-Kat seemed to have a penchant for shoes, and the ones she'd been wearing yesterday—which appeared to be the same ones on the film—were in a box on the top row. He slipped a pen through an ankle strap and lifted it for a closer look. They were fairly new, the matte leather barely creased at the stress points. The American size ten meant nothing to him, but he could tell it was a large shoe. But then again, Pussy-Kat was a woman of generous proportions—she needed a good foundation to support all that voluptuousness.

He spent a few seconds rummaging through boxes and flipping through her cramped wardrobe, careful to leave things as he'd found them. His hands stilled when he found the long coat in the back, half sticking out as if it had been hurriedly rehung. He quickly sifted through the pockets, but came up with only a movie ticket stub from several months ago and an opened roll of breath mints. The floppy hat was stuffed in the far corner but, again, yielded no hair or other physical evidence, so he stuffed it back.

And for a few seconds, he considered the impossible. If he disposed of the clothing, the evidence wouldn't be as overpowering. He shook his head to clear it—he was already treading on a thin professional line.

He then performed a perfunctory search of the living room, bathroom, and kitchen, again coming up empty-handed. James sighed, dreading the phone call to Lady Mercer, then wondered if Guy Trent had already contacted her.

Disgusted, James banged his hand on the white countertop. He was a weapons expert, a surveillance specialist, and a spy with a dozen aliases. In his twenty-year career with the British government, he'd protected statesmen, eluded assassins, extracted military secrets from various enemies, and freed heavily guarded hostages. And now after six months of retirement, he'd let a damn love letter slip through his fingers.

And an American woman slip into his heart.

He snorted in dismay, then retrieved the prized humidor and quietly took his leave.

"There, now, Katherine, what's all this nonsense about?"

At the sound of Valmer Getty's voice, Kat pushed her metal folding chair away from a wobbly wooden table and rushed into his arms. "Val! Thank God you're here."

The rotund trial lawyer hugged her hard, then held her at arm's length and gave her a wry smile. "My dear, when I said to call me sometime, I didn't mean from jail."

She tried to return the smile, but seeing her father's old friend brought back vivid memories of the last time she'd seen him—her father's funeral. Suddenly the full weight of the situation fell onto her shoulders, bowing them downward. "I'm in trouble, Val."

He looked behind him to make sure the door to the small room was closed, then patted her hand. "Start from the beginning," he said, then placed his briefcase on the table and removed his expensive suit jacket.

Kat glanced down and clasped her hands together tightly. "This started before Daddy died, Val."

The man frowned, pulling his lower lip into his mouth, then loosened his tie and pulled a rickety chair next to hers. "I'm a good listener."

"Ah, *Agent* Donovan." Detective Tenner, now in his shirtsleeves, acknowledged James's return to the gallery, escorted by Ronald Beaman. Apparently Tenner had passed some of the time delving into James's credentials. The inspector smirked. "And did Ms. McKray make it 'in one piece'?"

James cringed inwardly, but nodded pleasantly, realizing it was in Kat's best interests to get along with the man. Looking haggard, Guy Trent was seated in the aisle of a small cubicle nursing a cup of coffee. A digital clock on one of the desks read five thirty-five A.M. Tenner pulled two extra chairs to form a loose group around Guy and gestured for James to sit.

"Want some coffee?"

He had also assumed the role of gallant host, James noted. "No, thank you." Turning toward Guy Trent, James asked, "Have you contacted Lady Mercer?"

Guy shook his head. "Thought I'd wait until we had a few more details." His anger was clear with each perfectly enunciated word.

Tenner cleared his voice. "Plus Mr. Trent and Mr. Wharton discovered that a few more pieces are missing."

"Where is Mr. Wharton?" James asked, looking around. He wanted to talk to him too.

Guy waved vaguely toward the door. "Making arrangements to keep the museum closed today—you know, calling our ticket takers and guides to tell them not to come in. Plus it looks like we'll have to cancel the showing of the king's letter." Guy threw up his hands and glanced heavenward. "How could she do this to me?"

"What else is missing?" James asked, turning the chair around to straddle it.

Guy waved a sheet of ruled paper, then read, "A beaded Inca bracelet, two miniature Victorian oils, a ruby ring, and a gold compass." His entire head reddened, his eyes bulging. "They were probably taken because they're small pieces in larger collections spread out in the gallery—they wouldn't be easily missed."

James angled his head. "The tape didn't show the thief traipsing around the gallery picking up odds and ends."

Guy nodded, his lip curling. "I know. That's because Katherine probably took them sometime during the last few weeks. She could have smuggled them out in a pocket, a purse, anything."

"As could have anyone else," James pointed out.

"They're all pieces from Katherine's exhibits," Guy

said nastily. "It's her job to inventory the collections on a regular basis."

"Mr. Trent," James said carefully. "It's quite obvious to me that you and Ms. McKray have running disagreements. Are you sure you're not a little too anxious to pin these burglaries on her?"

Guy's mouth twisted in anger, then he took a deep breath. "Mr. Donovan, if I'm guilty of anything where Katherine is concerned, it's leniency. Several pieces have been stolen from the gallery this year, all of them small, all of them in Katherine's care."

James's heart twisted in alarm.

Tenner was writing furiously on a small pad. "Did you report the crimes, Mr. Trent?"

The little, round man shifted in his seat. "No."

Tenner's pen stopped. "No? Why not?"

Guy scrubbed his hand over his face and sighed wearily. "You have to understand our business, Mr. Tenner. Many galleries and art museums don't report stolen items because it's bad for the reputation of the showplace. Many of our collections are on loan. If word got out that our security was being compromised, we'd be blacklisted."

"Why then," James asked, "if you suspected Ms. McKray of stealing, did you not simply let her go?"

"Because at the time we thought it was a security guard, a man by the name of Jack Tomlin. I caught him once wearing a valuable piece of gallery jewelry. He said he was just trying it on, but I let him go." Guy shook his head. "Now I think I blamed the wrong person."

"What other items did Ms. McKray steal?" Tenner asked. James frowned at him and Tenner added, "Allegedly."

"Mostly small jewelry, and I distinctly remember a

valuable stamp disappeared. That sticks out in my mind because Katherine's father, Frank, was the one who found the stamp, at a junk dealer here in town. He bought it for fifteen dollars, and it was worth around fifteen thousand. Then a few weeks after Frank died," he snapped his fingers, "it vanished."

Tenner made a clicking sound with his tongue. "Frank McKray . . . I remember that case—ruled a suicide, wasn't it?"

James jerked his head up. *Suicide?*

Guy nodded slowly, his face grim. "It was a car accident, but everyone knew the truth." He stopped and exhaled noisily. "Frank worked for Jellico's for fifteen years—it was his life. He always thought he'd be made general manager one day, but when Mr. Jellico retired three years ago, he hired me."

"That would be Mr. Jellico, your brother-in-law?" James clarified.

Guy had the decency to blush. "Yes. Anyway, a year and a half ago, we were audited, and funds turned up missing from the gallery—tens of thousands of dollars. When the trail started leading back to Frank, he lost control. He was depressed, started drinking, even taking pills. He died before the investigation was complete."

"And had he embezzled funds?" James asked, thinking of the humidor filled with expensive, illegal cigars tucked away in his hotel room safe.

Guy nodded. "It appeared so. Katherine couldn't accept it, so she begged Mr. Jellico to let her pay back the money that was missing in exchange for keeping a lid on her father's activities."

"Did she pay it back?" Tenner asked, scribbling.

"Almost all of it, I believe, in regular payments and small lump sums. Only now that I think back, I'm wondering if she was stealing from the gallery to repay the debt." Guy Trent rose a bit unsteadily and excused himself to make a few phone calls.

Tenner had found another pack of gum somewhere and was intent on chewing it all at once. "Looks like this will be an open-and-shut case. Seems like such a waste— the woman's quite a looker, don't you think?"

James ignored him. As much as he hated to believe it, James had to admit that the evidence against Kat was growing. His gut instinct told him she was innocent, but had his judgment grown rusty?

FIVE

"Do you need a ride home?" Valmer held open the courtroom door and smiled in a way that reminded Kat of her father.

"I'll escort the lady home," a smooth, British voice said behind them.

Kat wheeled to see James leaning against an enormous marble pillar in the lobby of the government building. The late-afternoon sun slanted in, illuminating him from behind as he walked toward them. Her heart lifted involuntarily, but she noticed a slight frown on his brow. She felt ugly and plump in the clothes she'd been wearing for many hours, and her misery was only temporarily buoyed by being released on bond. She knew exhaustion lined her face.

James, on the other hand, looked like he'd just descended from a movie poster. Kat introduced the two men, amused that Valmer placed himself in front of her in a protective way.

"I'm not so sure Katherine should leave with you," Val said, puffing up his chest.

"It's okay, Val, he's a friend," she said, apprehensive about James's expression. Had he been unable to get the humidor? "I'll call you tomorrow morning," she promised, then gave the older man a squeeze. "How can I ever thank you?"

Val hugged her back. "By being very careful. Something fishy is going on, and I don't like it a bit."

She nodded and watched her father's friend walk away, then turned to James with a small smile. "How did you know where to find me?"

"I made a few phone calls," he said flatly. "My accent seems to break down barriers rather easily."

"Well . . . thanks."

He pursed his lips and swept a hand toward the lobby door. "Save your thanks until after we talk."

Kat descended the sweeping stone steps in silence, nervously wondering what her boss had told him. "Were you able to get the cigars?" she asked as they reached the sidewalk.

"They're safe," he said in a clipped tone, taking long strides toward his car parked a few yards away. James's face was stony as he opened the passenger door.

"You're angry with me," she said, facing him. "I'm sorry I asked you to help me, but I needed someone I could . . ." She trailed off, stopping short of using the word "trust." Was it trust, or was she so eager to buy into the glamour of a gorgeous, sexy, foreign agent coming to her rescue that she was throwing caution to the wind?

He leaned forward with agonizing slowness, until his eyes were level with hers. "Did you do it?" he asked quietly. His dark eyes bore into hers, commanding the truth.

Hurt that he suspected her sparked, then flamed in her breast. "No," she said through clenched teeth.

His eyebrows rose and relief eased his features, then he angled his head and asked, "Do I have your word, Pussy-Kat?"

His velvety voice rolled over her eardrums like a symphony, echoing deep inside her. Like her, he seemed to be struggling with a desire to trust. "Yes," she whispered. "I'm in a lot of trouble, aren't I?"

"Indeed," he acknowledged with a small nod. The lines of his face had softened. He reached forward and grazed her cheek with his balled fist. "But it's your own fault."

The touch of his hand sent her pulse racing. "*My* fault?"

His mouth curved into a warm smile that made her heart catch. "That's correct," he murmured. "If you had simply allowed me to spend the night, you would've had an airtight alibi—not to mention an unforgettable experience."

Absurdly heartened by the return of his good cheer, Kat smiled and swung into the seat. "Right now I'd settle for the alibi."

He adopted a hurt expression. "Once again you wound me, Ms. McKray." Then he winked and stepped back to close her door.

Unfamiliar feelings raged in her chest as Kat watched him walk around the car. His body moved with offhand athleticism in gray wool slacks, black turtleneck, and black cashmere jacket. He looked sleek and dangerous as he slid behind the wheel. After he pulled away from the curb, he glanced at her pointedly. "Were you treated well?"

She nodded. "I suppose, although I have no other experiences to compare with this one."

"Don't think I haven't been concerned," he said kindly, "but I spent most of the day at the gallery, trying to glean as much information as possible about the break-in."

Weariness pulled her head back on the leather seat. "This situation is so unbelievable, I don't know how to sort it all out."

"You could begin by telling me about the circumstances surrounding your father's death."

She was grateful for his careful tone, for treading softly on her loss. "He didn't kill himself, no matter what anyone says."

"And what about the embezzling?"

"Never," she whispered fiercely. "Dad could never have stolen from the gallery. He loved Jellico's—it was his life."

"Could he have reacted to being overlooked for the general manager position?"

Kat bit her bottom lip. "He was hurt—devastated even—when Mr. Jellico brought in Guy, but they acknowledged Dad's value to the gallery and gave him a hefty raise. He was content, if not entirely happy." She blinked back hot tears.

"So if you believe him innocent, why are you paying back the money?"

Embarrassment shot through her and she averted her eyes. "I see Guy has been spilling his guts."

"He thinks you're guilty."

"He's a moron."

"Tenner believes him."

"Then he's a moron too."

James laughed, a low, pleasing sound. "So why?"

Kat lifted her chin. "Keeping my dad's name clear was the last thing I could do for him."

He pressed his lips together. "Mr. Trent said you've nearly paid it back."

Satisfaction warmed her. "In another couple of months it'll be paid in full, with interest. Forty-four thousand, six hundred fifty-two dollars." It was probably a paltry amount to James, but it was a considerable sum to her.

"I suspect San Francisco is an expensive place to live. How did you manage?"

"A ridiculous amount is deducted from my paycheck, and I make extra payments when I can." She choked out a bitter laugh. "I was planning to resign on the day I made the last payment."

"They made you stay at Jellico's as part of the deal?"

Her lips formed a straight, hard line. "That's right."

"That borders on extortion."

She shrugged. "I suppose. But Jellico's is a prestigious gallery, so I'm getting good experience. Make that past tense—I'm sure I'm fired."

"Your boss implied that you'd gotten the money for extra payments by selling items stolen from the gallery."

Kat scoffed and pushed her hands toward him, palm up. "I earned the money for extra payments by refinishing antiques for people who are too rich to get their own hands dirty. See—my hands are permanently stained mahogany number twenty-seven."

He captured her left hand in his right one, snatching her breath as well. His thumb massaged her palm. The interior of the car hummed with tension. "Then if your father didn't take the money, and you didn't steal the pieces, who is menacing the gallery?"

She stared down at their hands, settled on the console between them. Her nipples hardened with every stroke of his thumb. "I-I honestly don't know who took the money, but I think my father had his theories."

"He never told you?"

She shook her head, overwhelmed with regret. "I knew something was bothering him, but I didn't know anything about the embezzlement allegations until after he'd died. Mr. Jellico and Guy called me in, and we struck the deal."

"Who was working for the gallery at the time the money showed up missing?"

"All of us, plus Mr. Jellico's wife when we had special events. She's deceased now. There are two part-time accountants who were with us then, but they were cleared. Gloria Handelman worked in administration for a couple of months—she's the daughter of a rich collector in town." A thought struck her and she gasped. "This may be off the subject, but the Handelmans were going to bid on the king's letter."

His head swung in her direction. "Would she know the gallery well enough to pull off a heist?"

"With my security badge, sure."

James pursed his lips and nodded. "Sounds like a good lead. What about the things missing from the gallery over the past year?"

"That may not be as much of a conspiracy as Guy thinks it is," she said, lifting her shoulders. "On some days we have hundreds of visitors—"

"They detected four more items this morning."

Kat frowned. "What things?"

"Jewelry, a gold compass, two miniature oils—"

She winced. "The Victorian oils?"

"I think so."

"Oh, those were part of my favorite exhibit."

"Mr. Trent mentioned it was your exhibit, as was every other exhibit with items missing."

She sighed. "James, every exhibit in the gallery is *my* exhibit. That's my job."

"So were the paintings there when you left last night?"

Closing her eyes, she tried to concentrate. She remembered making rounds after James and Mr. Muldoon had left, around four-thirty. But a group of patrons had been gathered around the collection of twelve miniatures. She'd stopped to chat a minute, and one of the volunteers had asked a question about the pigments used in the paints of that period.

"They were still on display around four forty-five, but I can't swear to it after that." She looked at James and shrugged slightly. "James, you're probably accustomed to high-profile, intricate cases, but the embezzling, the missing items, and the theft of the letter could be unrelated."

"True," he acknowledged with an air that made her feel as though she was missing something that was quite obvious to him.

He withdrew his hand to parallel park near her apartment door. She missed his warmth, and it disturbed her. "Oh, I was going to ask you to drop me by the gallery to get my van."

"The police towed it."

Kat stared at him. "You're kidding."

"Evidence," he said, turning off the engine. "And prepare yourself—I'm sure they've searched your apartment by now."

She gripped the handle. "Look, James, I'm sure you're exhausted from your trip and today's activities—"

He stopped her with a pointed look. "I've never suffered from jet lag in my life, and we have many things to discuss. Plus I want to see you safely secured away."

Relief washed over her, and she supposed her face showed it. "I'd be grateful."

He froze, then leaned toward her, his eyes glinting in amusement. "Grateful, did you say?"

His gaze roved over her, and Kat burned with embarrassment. The man must have an indiscriminate taste for American women if he could flirt with her the way she looked now. She fumbled for the door handle and nearly tripped in her haste to escape his close proximity. By the time she had righted herself, he was out of the car and beside her, taking her arm.

"Easy," he said, his voice as soothing as the hot shower she intended to take the instant he left. And as far as these weird, tingly feelings James evoked in her, she passed it off as lack of sleep, lack of food, and lack of sex.

Her shoulders tensed as they climbed the few steps and walked down the hall. When he swung open the door, she thought she was prepared for the worst, but she was wrong.

"Bloody hell," he muttered.

Vile American words whirled through Kat's head, but her tongue and body were paralyzed. She recognized the arm of her couch peeking out beneath a mountain of books and other debris. Drawers and shelves had been emptied, with no thought to replacing the items. Scarcely a bare spot remained on the floor. Pots and pans, bathroom linens, clothing—the contents of the rooms had been commingled and abandoned.

She lifted her hand to her mouth and whispered, "Can they do this?"

"Apparently so," James replied, lifting a carbon of a written order that had been taped to the door. He swung his head back and forth to survey the damage. "Seems a bit sloppy to me."

Kat's legs felt rubbery. In the space of a few seconds, the events of the last twenty-four hours had caught up to her.

He curled his arm around her waist. "You're quite pale, Pussy-Kat, maybe you'd better lie down."

Which seemed like the most hilarious thing she'd ever heard, considering there was no place for her to lie down. She opened her mouth to laugh, but only a pathetic little squeak emerged.

James released her and removed his jacket, hanging it from a bare nail where a picture had once hung, then began rolling up his sleeves. "I'll clear us a spot to sit while you freshen up," he said cheerfully.

She smoothed a hand down the sleeve of the ratty cardigan she'd thrown on over her dinner clothes—God, had it been only this morning? Her skin itched, her scalp crawled, her tongue tasted stale. Her state of grooming seemed insignificant compared to everything else she'd been through, but right now the small solace of hot water sounded like nirvana. "Well, perhaps just a quick shower," she murmured.

He waved her toward the bedroom, then began retrieving books from the sofa and shelving them. Kat yanked a semi-folded towel from a mound on the floor and walked into the disaster area that used to be her bedroom. Swallowing a lump of frustration, she marched straight through the strewn articles of her life and into the white tiled bathroom, which was too small for the police to have wrought much damage. At least the shower curtain hung intact.

She turned on the water and let it run over her fingers until it warmed. Kat stole a glance toward the living room, then slowly pulled the bathroom door shut. Every nerve ending, every muscle quivered as she undressed, keenly aware of the man only a few strides away.

A stranger, really. Handsome, aloof, confident, oozing more testosterone than all the men she'd been complaining about to Denise yesterday at lunch put together. How had they become so . . . so . . . *comfortable* that she had relaxed her normal paranoid security measures where people, and especially men, were concerned?

She unbound her hair and stared at the lock on the bathroom door. It had never worked. Was she being foolishly trustworthy? She had never even seen the man's identification—she'd taken him at his word that he was some kind of secret service man for the crown, or something like that. Walking into the shower backward, she jerked the curtain shut.

Kat reached for the shampoo and dumped a glob on the top of her head. Where exactly had Agent Donovan been during the burglary? If anyone in the group could get around security measures, it would be he. Perhaps his scam was accompanying a piece of art to its destination, then stealing it and selling it on the black market. He'd make money, the owner would collect insurance. . . .

Lathering her hair furiously, she mulled over what she knew about him. If he *was* a secret agent, then he probably knew all kinds of ways to kill people. Plus, how to make it appear accidental. And if he worked for the British government, he probably had diplomatic immunity—a license to thrill, er . . . kill.

At the sound of a muffled thump, she jerked up her head. What was that? Had he barricaded them inside the apartment? Would he hold her hostage? Make her bend to his sexual will? She sounded hysterical, even to herself, but she couldn't stop the rush of adrenaline. She had to get out of here.

Rinsing her hair frantically, she remembered his gun—and God only knew how many other weapons he carried: poison-tipped writing pens, detonating jewelry, a switchblade.

The scene from *Psycho* flashed through her mind and she looked around quickly for something to use in her defense if he came crashing through the door. A rusty disposable razor lay in the corner—she could nick him to death and hope for tetanus.

Kat soaped and rinsed her skin in mere seconds, then turned off the water with shaky hands and wrapped the towel around her. After hurriedly wringing the moisture from her hair, she listened carefully at the bathroom door. Nothing.

No, wait . . . something.

Music?

Kat recognized the crashing, grinding crescendos of the instrumental theme to a live performance she'd seen. From all the CDs she owned that were probably scattered to the four corners of the apartment, he'd somehow managed to find her favorite.

Opening the door a crack, she peeked into her bedroom. Not only was the coast clear, but it appeared he had closed the door leading into the living room to give her privacy. Was it possible that she had met the last breathing gentleman on earth? Then she recalled his wicked innuendos and decided that James Donovan was only a gentleman when it suited his purposes.

After hunting for toiletries and coming up empty-handed except for a bottle of pink baby lotion, she sat down on her clothes-covered bed and massaged the creamy stuff into her skin. The colossal mess in her room made her sick to her stomach. Or was that hunger? The clock read five-fifteen and she hadn't eaten since last night's white lasagna. She mined underwear, a pair of gray leggings, and a long white shirt from the mountains of clothing on her bed and dresser. It would take her days to get things back in place. And it took every ounce of energy she had to keep from stretching out on the floor on top of her sock collection and screaming.

Her hair dryer was nowhere to be found, so she simply combed her long wet hair straight back from her forehead. She did, however, find her ancient fuzzy house shoes. Pulling them on felt like hugging an old friend. Today, she was taking pleasure wherever she could find it.

Kat paused for a moment inside her bedroom door, smiling wryly at her earlier wild musings. So James was a little forward, a little too confident, a little overwhelming . . . that was a long way from being a criminal.

A knock on the other side startled her. "Kat?" he asked, his voice low.

Instead of worrying like a ninny, she should be thankful to have someone of his expertise on her side. How that could have come about was a bit of a mystery in and of itself. She turned the knob and opened the door, poised to thank James for everything he'd done.

Instead, she froze at the butcher knife he held toward her chest.

SIX

"Are you hungry?" James asked, confused at the expression on her face. "I ordered in a pizza pie."

"P-Pizza?" she asked, eyeing the knife warily.

He glanced at the knife in his hand and laughed. "I couldn't locate the correct tool to cut it, so I improvised."

She smiled shakily and nodded, then looked over his shoulder. "It smells wonderful."

Not nearly as wonderful as she smelled, he noted, his body tightening in response to the sweet, fresh scent floating around her. He'd had to close the door to her bedroom and turn on the stereo to drown out the sounds of her showering. Had Kat's life not been turned upside down in the past few hours, he might have joined her, the desire to see her lush curves shiny-slick almost embarrassing for a man who prided himself on self-control. He swept his arms toward the small kitchen. "I found two barstools and cleared enough counter space for us to eat."

She ran her fingers through her dark, wet hair, disrupting the even marks her comb had left behind. Without her glasses, she seemed softer, more vulnerable. The lady had exceptional skin, pale without makeup, but wonderfully translucent. And the kind of bone structure that guaranteed her graceful aging. She walked in front of him, picking her way around the mess, and he noticed her house slippers.

"Fond of those furry feet-things, aren't you?" he asked, not bothering to hide his amusement.

"Love me, love my slippers," she quipped, the mere mention of the *l* word causing his heart to temporarily seize. "How did you know to order from Sid's?" she asked, raising the lid on the pizza box. "Oooh, olives." She lifted out a slice of the cheese-gooey pizza and bit off the pointed end with nice, even teeth.

"It's listed on your phone's speed dial directory," he said, pointing to the device he'd unearthed in the couch cushions. "By the way, your message light is flashing."

Still chewing, she walked over and punched a button. The voice reported she had five messages. Kat glanced at James, a slight frown furrowing her brow. She was weighing whether to trust him with her personal communication. He busied himself with removing two beers from her refrigerator, his gaze averted, but his ears pricked. A high-pitched tone sounded, then Denise's voice came on the line.

"Kat, call me when you get home—I want to hear all about your date with Mister Divine." James bit back a smile, and resisted looking in Kat's direction for her reaction. Another tone sounded. "Ms. McKray," a female voice said, "this is Maria Russert from Channel Thirty-one news. We'd like an interview about the theft at the gallery."

Kat must have cut her off, because another tone

sounded. "Kat, this is Guy." His voice was brusque, a shade short of rude. "Under the circumstances, I think it would be best for all involved if you took an indefinite leave of absence. Call and leave a voice message to let me know you received this." James winced—not unexpected, but still another blow for her to deal with.

Another tone, and Denise's voice again, this time several octaves higher. "Kat! Jesus Christ Almighty, where are you? I heard on the news that the gallery was burglarized, and when I called you at work, some dumbass told me you'd been arrested! I'm having congestive heart failure! Call me the *instant* you get this message." Another tone, and Denise's voice again, this time a frantic whisper. "Kat! The police were just here asking me all kinds of questions about you! What the freak is going on? I'm going nutso waiting to hear from you!"

After a few seconds of silence, James lifted his head and chanced a glance in her direction. She had abandoned her pizza and stood holding the handset, her fingers poised to dial. "James," she said, swinging her face toward him, "I need to make a couple of quick phone calls."

"Would you like some privacy?" he felt obliged to ask.

But she was already dialing. She paused a moment, apparently waiting for a recorder to kick on. "Guy, this is Katherine. I received your message, and I agree with you one hundred percent. I'll be in touch." He admired how direct and strong her voice sounded. Kat dialed again, her face brightening after a few seconds. "Hey, Denise, it's me. Yeah, can you believe it—they even handcuffed me. . . . Well, of course I didn't do it. . . ." She put one hand on her hip. "Denise, what time did you leave last night? Nine-thirty? Are you absolutely sure? Okay. Did anyone call or did you notice anyone hanging around last night when you left?" She bit her lower lip, frowning. "Did anyone come to the door—a salesman perhaps? Because some maniac got in here and stole my clothes and security badge, then dressed up like me to break into a vault. . . . No, Denise, I'm not shitting you." She smiled wryly in James's direction. "I'll be fine—Valmer Getty is handling everything. . . . Yes . . . er, no, don't come over." She looked at James again, this time shifting uncomfortably. "Mr. Donovan drove me home." Kat sighed. "Yes, he's still here."

Cupping the mouthpiece with her hand, she turned her back and lowered her voice. He almost couldn't hear her. Almost. "It's not like that, Denise. . . . I'm hanging up now. . . . I will. . . . You have a very dirty mind. . . . I promise. . . . Good-bye." She clamped the phone down, then turned a cheery smile in his direction. "How about that? I'm fired and the police shook down my best friend."

He nodded and lowered himself to a barstool, dubiously studying the greasy pizza pie before transferring a slice to a paper towel. "How well do you know your friend Denise?" Experimentally he bit off a small chunk, then took a larger bite.

Kat rescued her own dinner from the end table and joined him at the bar, shoving aside a haphazard stack of cereal boxes. "We've been friends for three years—what are you getting at?"

James shrugged casually at her prickly response. "I'm just trying to rule out possible suspects. She was here and could easily have taken your clothing and badge."

"You don't know Denise," she said, shaking her head.

"People can behave strangely if they are desperate," he pressed. "Is she in financial straits?"

"No," she said quickly, then stopped. "Well, except for joking about money to buy her apartment—her building is being converted to condos."

"Is she familiar with the gallery?"

Frowning, Kat angled her head at him. "Several weeks ago she asked me to take her on a full-blown tour. I showed her the vaults that day." Her voice had grown much more uncertain, then she straightened. "Denise couldn't—wouldn't—do it."

"Could she be an unwitting accomplice, perhaps giving someone else access to your place without your knowledge, or even hers? A boyfriend perhaps?"

"I think she's seeing someone, but she insists he's just a friend."

"Do you know his name?"

"No, but this is a stretch, James, don't you think?"

"Does she know the circumstances surrounding your employment with Jellico's?"

She fidgeted. "No."

"Then if you have secrets from her, don't you think it likely that she has secrets from you?"

She shook her head stubbornly. "I can't comprehend it."

"Okay," he relented for the time being, taking a swig of the weak domestic beer. "Then let's go down the list: Who would want to frame you?"

She sighed mightily and lifted her hands palm up. "If I knew that, Agent Donovan, don't you think I would have been shouting it from the top of the jailhouse?"

At last the color returned to her cheeks. She was, he decided, simply beautiful. Tumble-out-of-bed-looking-great beautiful. Her expressive brows held her looks just

shy of classic—her features were unique, arresting . . .
and had become alarmingly satisfying to his eyes in a
short period of time. He blinked, forcing his attention
back to the matter at hand. "What about your boss? Or
even his boss? Perhaps this is a way to get rid of you
since your so-called debt to them is nearly paid."

Kat pushed back a long lock of dark hair that had
dried and fallen over her ear. "I suspect that Guy knew
I'd be leaving soon—they weren't going to have to push
me out the door. Remember, they're the ones who
wanted this working arrangement, not me. Besides, Guy
was so excited about showing the king's love letter, he'd
never do anything to jeopardize the show. I'm sure he's
devastated."

"Does the gallery specialize in private auctions?"

She shook her head, dislodging more thick hair to
distract him. "No, in fact, this is the first auction to
attract media attention at Jellico's. We typically give the
pieces West Coast coverage, then ship them back east to
the large auction houses."

"And how did the gallery learn about the letter?"

"Guy has European connections from a Los Angeles
gallery he ran before coming to Jellico's. Since there are
several document collectors in the Bay Area, he's con-
stantly putting out feelers for new entries on the market."

"These document collectors—are they history
buffs?"

She lifted the bottle of beer to her mouth for a quick
drink. "Not necessarily—we've sold letters, movie
scripts, autographs, even recipes."

He pursed his lips. "I suppose there is a market for
everything. What about the other fellow, Wharton?"

She dismissed his notion with a wave. "Andy's harmless. He's quite a good painter, studied all over Europe, but in this city, good painters are a dime a dozen. He turned his talents toward restoration, and my dad hired him while I was working summers during college."

"Are you artistic?" he probed.

This prompted a laugh, a sound he definitely wanted to hear more often. "I was only blessed with an appreciation and a good eye."

"So you're good at what you do?" He hadn't meant it to be a loaded question, but the glance she gave him said she suspected a setup.

"Yes," she said simply. "Otherwise, Guy wouldn't tolerate me working there, no matter how much he thought I owed the gallery. For all his faults, he runs a top-notch operation." She took another bite, twisting the stretchy cheese around a finger and licking it off.

James ran a finger around the collar of his turtleneck. "What about the security officers?"

Kat chewed slowly as she pondered his question. "Carl Jays and Ronald Beaman are the only ones I know past a first-name basis. Ron has been with the gallery since the day it opened and, as far as I know, has never raised an eyebrow."

"Mr. Trent mentioned a guard he fired because he suspected the man of stealing."

Nodding, Kat said, "I remember, but I think Guy was wrong. Jack Tomlin was guilty of overly admiring some of the gallery's jewelry, but I don't believe he was a thief."

He mentally ticked down the growing list of suspects. "You trust everyone, don't you, Pussy-Kat?"

Kat's breath caught at the pet name he bandied about with such ease. It was obvious he'd spent a lifetime perfecting flirtation. How many women had fallen victim to his charms? What shocked her the most was that she could sit here and logically analyze his methods, yet still be affected by them like a uniformed schoolgirl.

Her hand tightened around the cold bottle she held. "No, I don't trust everyone, Mr. Donovan. While we're on the subject, where were you last night at twelve-thirty?"

His black eyebrows climbed his smooth forehead. "Would you believe reflecting on our missed, ahem, opportunity?"

Her pulse vaulted. "Not for a second."

Shrugging gallantly, he pulled a wry grin. "I decided to postpone my flight until today, so I checked into a hotel, watched some horrible TV interview shows, and tried to rest. I finally gave up and drove around the city for a while, then ended up back at the gallery. You know the rest."

"So you were alone the entire time?" she asked, thinking it very likely he could have picked up someone in the hotel bar—an image which bothered her immensely.

One corner of his mouth lifted. "Unfortunately, yes, I was alone."

Faintly relieved, Kat crossed her arms triumphantly. "It seems your alibi is about as airtight as mine, Agent Donovan."

He spread his hands wide. "But what motive would I have?"

Kat angled her head at him. "Money?"

"I don't need it."

She thought about the remarks he'd made concerning the letter's owner, Lady Mercer. "Love?"

James's brown eyes widened, then he shook his head with deliberate slowness. "Not in my vocabulary."

Intrigued, Kat filed away his response. "Just for the thrill of it?"

He caught her gaze, then leaned forward on his stool until his face was only inches from hers.

Kat froze, unable to look away, appalled at her thrashing heart. The man's senses were so superhuman, he could probably hear it.

His eyes sparkled with warmth and humor, and his mouth was drawn back, revealing both dimples. His breath feathered across her chin three times before he smiled and said, "I'd rather get my thrills taking things which are freely given."

Her pulse and the music from the stereo pounded in her ears. Her throat constricted, forcing her to swallow, painfully and audibly.

He reached forward in slow motion until he touched her cheek with his warm forefinger. Kat's eyes closed involuntarily, her mind spun, her lips opened a fraction.

"You," he whispered, "look good enough to eat."

She opened her eyes as his finger swept a tiny semicircle against her skin.

"Even without pizza sauce on your face." His grin widened, revealing white teeth. A splash of red sauce decorated his long finger.

Embarrassment bolted through her and she pulled back, patting the counter for a napkin, then wiped her face as he laughed heartily.

"You could have said something," she murmured.

"I did," he said, his full-throated mirth surrounding her.

At last, she gave in to the mood and smiled, then joined in his laughter. Shaking her head, she pushed herself up. "Would you like another beer?"

"No offense," he said, palming his empty bottle, "but American beer is a bit watered down for my tastes."

"I have white wine." She looked around the jumbled kitchen. "Somewhere."

"Thanks all the same," he said, standing up. "What can I do to help?"

Kat started to protest, then relented. Telling herself she could use the help and ignoring the nagging feeling that she wanted to prolong his visit, she said, "Well I can't get everything back in its place tonight—you ought to see my bedroom."

"If you insist," he said cheerfully, capturing her wrist and turning in the direction of her room.

Her heart thudded in alarm—she was getting in over her head with this English Casanova. "B-But the kitchen would be a good place to start," she said, standing her ground and twisting out of his hold. "All the dishes will have to be cleaned—God knows who handled them. Will you hand me plates to fill the dishwasher?"

He sighed, but relented with a slight bow. "At your service."

She opened the machine to find a few unwashed items, her eyes drawn immediately to two green-patina coffee mugs in the top rack. "That's odd," she said, picking up one of them.

"What?"

"I didn't use these coffee cups."

He frowned. "Someone did."

"Do you suppose the policemen used them—perhaps for a drink out of the tap?" She lifted the cup and inhaled a deep, slightly acrid odor. "No, this one had coffee in it." Claiming the other one and turning it over, she announced, "This one too."

"I doubt they would have made themselves coffee," James said. "What about your friend?"

Kat glanced up in surprise. "Denise?"

"Perhaps she had a guest over, after all."

For the first time, Kat experienced misgivings about her girlfriend. "I'll just call and ask her." She replaced the coffee mugs, only to have James reach past her with a handkerchief to retrieve them and set them on the counter.

"Possible evidence," he explained. "And postpone ringing her until I can do some checking into Miss Womack's background."

"You can do that?"

James pursed his lips and nodded.

"On anyone?"

Another nod.

"What could you find out?" she asked, intrigued and perturbed. "About someone like me, for instance."

"If I invested some time," he said with a small shrug, "practically anything—the places you shop, the things you buy, the man you're sleeping with."

Kat laughed nervously, gesturing for him to hand her a stack of mismatched, brightly colored plates. "Well, if you find out, I want to be the first to know his name."

"Ah, no boyfriend?" He handed her a yellow and orange plate, his expression surprised.

"Not currently," she supplied self-consciously. Not for ages, really, but he didn't need to know.

"No aspirations for a family? Little Pussy-Kittens, perhaps?"

He'd hit a nerve, but he didn't need to know that either. Kat attributed her longing for children and a family of her own to losing her parents and having no siblings with whom to share the loss. "It would be hard to raise children in the state penitentiary," she said, trying to lighten the mood.

"So you *do* want children." His voice rose with new insight and he grinned as he handed her a pink and turquoise plate.

"I don't dwell on it," she said wryly. "How about you?"

Confusion crossed his brow and he averted his eyes. "I never allowed myself to think about it before, due to the nature of my job."

The domesticity of their situation struck her—standing in the kitchen putting away dishes and talking about having a family. "And now?" she prompted.

He brightened, his self-assurance returned. "And now I quite like the freedom of traveling to foreign countries and meeting charming women like yourself."

So he was either a confirmed bachelor or loosely committed to the woman in England. "And does Lady Mercer share your enthusiasm for your spreading good cheer to women of the world?"

"Tania?"

From the expression on his face, she knew if he were loosely committed to anyone, it was not the Mercer woman.

"I respect Lady Mercer for certain of her, um"—he cleared his throat—"qualities, but I assure you our relationship is strictly business."

Kat cocked an eyebrow. "No assurance needed, Mr. Donovan, I was simply being conversational."

"Well then," he said, spreading his arms wide, "for conversation's sake, I'm an unfettered man."

"And have you spoken with Lady Mercer since the break-in?"

His smile disappeared. "She was out, so I shared the

turn of events with her assistant. But I left word not to worry—we'll find the thief and the missing letter. And the whole episode will probably fetch her even more money in the auction."

"Probably," Kat agreed as she racked more plates, then pointed to the saucers. "But I wish I were so certain the police will find the burglar."

"I didn't say the police," he corrected. "Detective Tenner is quite content to believe that you stole the letter and the other pieces from the gallery. Which means," he said with a smile, "the real perpetrator thinks he or she is off the hook. Which means we can catch them off guard."

"We?" Kat asked.

"As in you and me," he affirmed. "I'd never forgive myself if an innocent woman were locked up and denied the chance to have a cottage full of children."

Kat frowned at a chipped saucer and set it aside. "I'm sorry for the delay in your trip to New York. I know this has turned out to be more than you bargained for."

"An understatement of gigantic proportions," he said softly. Kat glanced up and reached for a red saucer he held out to her, but when she curled her fingers around it, he refused to relinquish his grip. Instead he plucked the saucer from her hand and clasped her wrist, then pulled her toward him slowly, as if he expected her to resist.

She didn't. What woman could? He was irresistible, a larger-than-life image, a devastatingly sexy, charming superhero who seemed—at least for this moment—to want her. She had never felt more secure and desirable. Kat became fluid in his arms, her curves surging against the hard planes of his body. He wrapped his arms around her and lowered his mouth with hard and fast intent. She held him loosely at first, tightening her hold around his neck as the urgency of their kiss increased.

His lips were soft, but demanding. He stole her breath into his mouth in great gulps, and she gasped for air between the clashing of their tongues, their teeth. The bittersweet taste of beer remained on his tongue, and Kat lapped it up, echoing his moans.

James crushed her against him, his hands roaming freely down her back and over her hips. Desire exploded low in her stomach and flamed out to her limbs as she felt his need for her growing hard against her belly. Reason fled, and all that mattered was his hands on her body.

He slid his hands under her shirt and explored her like a lost traveler looking for home, his fingers searching, finding, revering. Her breasts bloomed as he caressed them through her satiny bra, teasing the peaks until her arms weakened and dropped to his waist. She kneaded his back muscles through the thin fabric of his shirt, pressing herself into his hands, opening her mouth to his plundering tongue. His groans resonated in her throat, sending a hum through her limbs.

As he slipped the strap of her bra down one shoulder, he rained kisses along her jaw, triggering waves of shuddering desire. She rolled her shoulders, arching to meet him as his mouth traveled to her neck. He gently nipped at her lobe and flicked his tongue over the shell of her ear, sending liquid heat through her midsection and arrowing down to her thighs.

"Miss McKray," he whispered between ragged breaths, "I should very much like to inspect the condition of your bedroom."

SEVEN

Ten heart-pounding, flesh-grinding, bone-melting seconds passed before his words sank in and sanity returned. Kat froze and her eyes popped open.

James, sensing her withdrawal, increased the urgency of his caresses, and crooned into her ear, "On the other hand, the sofa would serve us just as well." He urged her to follow him, but at her resistance, he lifted his head.

Kat disentangled herself and righted her clothes, her mind spinning. Ignoring the disappointment and longing surging through her body, she took a deep breath and gasped, "James, having sex is not going to help anything."

Hands on hips, James glanced down at the bulge straining the front of his slacks and grinned wryly. "I'm afraid I don't concur."

She averted her eyes and backed away from him, trying to rid herself of the lingering burn of his hands on her skin. Gesturing around the room, she laughed wildly. "Look at this place—this represents the state of my life right now, and you want us to get naked!"

His eyebrows went up in the middle to form an inverted V. "You seemed to be enjoying it as much as I, Pussy-Kat."

A hot flush spread over her face. "I . . . I lost my head. I'm sorry if I gave you the wrong impression. It's been a crazy day, and I'm not myself."

He slowly dragged his fingers through his hair, exhaling. "Forgive me—I don't make a habit of taking advantage of damsels in distress."

Part of her felt flattered that he seemed so disappointed, but a larger part felt annoyed at his inference that she needed to be rescued. Her chin came up. "And I don't make a habit of *being* a damsel in distress."

James sighed. "Once again I offend you," he said, splaying his hands. "Perhaps we should both get some rest and resume work on the case tomorrow. I'll drop the cups off to the detective before I return to my hotel." He walked over to the counter and carefully wrapped the two coffee mugs in paper towels.

Barbs of remorse pricked Kat—she didn't want him to leave, and that in itself scared her almost as much as the prospect of going to jail for something she didn't do. She found a plastic grocery bag and held it open in silence as he lowered the cups into it. Her mind raced for healing words, but as she opened her mouth, a knock sounded at her door. She jumped at the noise, her nerves a jangled mess.

"Are you expecting anyone?"

Kat shook her head and walked to the door, wondering what else could happen today. "Who is it?"

"It's Valmer, Katherine."

Her shoulders eased forward in relief and she swung open the door. "Come in, Val."

"How are you doing, my dear?" Still dressed in his

suit, the rotund man stopped when he noticed James, then addressed him, his voice tinged with suspicion. "I thought you were simply driving Katherine home, Mr. Donovan."

James nodded, then indicated her apartment with his arm. "When we discovered this mess, I helped her straighten up a bit and we ordered in."

Feeling guilty and exposed without her glasses and with her hair hanging loose around her shoulders, Kat was too aware of the hot flush climbing her neck. Valmer glanced back and forth between them—he obviously suspected hanky-panky.

"Has there been a new development?" James stepped in smoothly to bridge the awkward moment.

Val turned back to Kat. "I thought you'd want to know the grand jury will hear your case in one week."

Her knees felt rubbery, so she sat down hard on the denim couch. "As of now, what are the chances that I'll be indicted?"

Val's grunt was not comforting. "Well, it's all circumstantial evidence, but it's strong. I'd say fifty-fifty, but you could shift the odds in your favor if you take a lie detector test."

Kat's heart pounded and she glanced up nervously at James, then back to Val. "Is that necessary?"

"It would help, Kat, and it's a fairly simple procedure."

Dread mushroomed in her stomach. "What kind of questions will I be asked?"

"Simple things to set the baseline for your responses," he said, "with inquiries about the burglary thrown in at intervals." He walked over and patted her shoulder. "Don't worry, you'll do just fine. We'll beat these charges, Katherine."

She conjured up a brave smile. "Of course we will."

James briefed Valmer about the possible significance of the coffee cups and told him he would hand-deliver them to Detective Tenner.

"Perhaps I'd better take them," Val offered hesitantly, still unconvinced of James's trustworthiness.

"Be my guest," James said magnanimously, pushing the bag toward him. "But I plan to see him regardless."

Val's mouth twisted. "I'll call Detective Tenner tomorrow morning to make sure he received them." Turning to go, he said, "Call me in the morning to set up a time for the polygraph, okay, Kat?"

She stood on shaky legs and walked the few steps to the door with him. "Val, what if I'm nervous? What if I fail the test?"

He smiled, revealing white dentures. "You won't—everything will be fine, Katherine. You'll see." Then he squeezed her hand and closed the door behind him.

Kat held on to the doorknob and kept her back to James, trying to regain her composure. Her body was still rebounding from her lapse with James, and now she had one more setback to cinch a sleepless night: She would never pass the polygraph. One impulsive sin would come back to haunt her.

James studied her from behind, the droop of her shoulders, the white-knuckled grip on the doorknob. Offering comfort to her seemed like the most natural thing in the world. Walking up behind her, he gently wrapped his arms around her, covered her hands with his, and dropped his chin to her shoulder. Her hair smelled heavenly, and that sweet, soft smell lingered on her skin. She acknowledged his presence by relaxing into him slightly. When he could no longer will his body to remain calm, he whispered, "I'll call you early tomorrow."

James reluctantly released her and she moved away from the door to open it. While shrugging into his jacket, he winked at her, glad to see her mouth turn up slightly at the corners. He didn't want to leave her alone, and the revelation stunned him. "I'll come back to stay if you need company," he offered. "I'll take the sofa."

"No," she said softly. "I don't think that would be wise."

He pursed his lips, nodding in agreement. "Okay, call me at the Flagiron Hotel if you require my services—" He paused and searched for firmer ground, "That is, if you wish to speak to me."

She smiled, but the spark didn't reach her blue eyes, which seemed a little too wide and a little too moist for his comfort.

James walked to his car in the early dusk of the evening, passing off his antsy feelings as simple pent-up lust. Kat was a beautiful, desirable woman in trouble, and he was programmed to offer assistance. It was natural to have protective feelings for her—but these strange sensations rumbling around in his chest felt alien to him.

Then he grinned wryly. Perhaps it was his ego smarting from being turned down for the first time in his life. He seemed to be losing his touch in several areas.

James headed to the police station and circled for thirty minutes to find a parking place, then entered the nondescript building and asked an officer seated behind bulletproof glass for Detective Tenner. The uniformed man waved him through a door where he patted James down. He warned him of the gun before the officer found it, then presented various credentials and licenses. The officer also searched the bag containing the two cups, adding his own prints before James could stop him. Finally satisfied, the man checked his weapon and gave him vague directions, sending James on a journey through a noisy maze of cubicles and people, a hodgepodge of police officers, suspects, and witnesses.

Incredibly, he heard the snapping gum before he found the detective. Tenner was sitting on a desk, his feet in a chair, his grubby white shirtsleeves rolled up to the elbows. The tie was long gone, it seemed. He stopped mid-laugh in response to something a seated companion was saying.

"Weeellll, Agent Donovan," he said, then kicked the chair out of the way and lurched to his feet. "What brings you here?"

James nodded his greeting. "I was wondering if the lab reports are back on the coffee the security guards at Jellico's were drinking."

Tenner stretched out the gum with the tip of his tongue and squinted. James knew the tests had come back, but the detective was deliberating whether to tell him.

"You and I are on the same side, Detective," James assured him.

"Is that so?" the man asked, cocking his head. "Well, I think you've got a thing for that McKray woman."

James pursed his lips. "Which doesn't make her any more or less guilty, does it?"

"No," Tenner agreed, still dubious.

"The results have to be made available before the grand jury meets—what harm could it do to let me in on it? I'd like to keep my client in England informed of the progress of the case."

Tenner blew a bubble, then sucked it back into his mouth. "Over-the-counter sleeping pills in the coffee. Funny—they're the same brand as the ones we found in your girlfriend's nightstand."

His reference to their relationship rankled James, but he didn't react. "Which is still circumstantial," James pointed out. "What else did you find to warrant making such a mess?"

The detective grunted. "The coat, hat, and shoes."

James shrugged. "But you expected to, correct?"

"Yep, but we didn't plan on finding a piece of the gallery's missing jewelry."

The last bit of news startled James. "Jewelry, did you say?"

"Yep—a ring."

"Where?"

Tenner shook his head smugly. "I think I'll keep that one to myself."

James's pulse jumped and he experienced a twinge of doubt. Was it possible Kat had taken the jewelry? She had seemed very concerned about passing the polygraph. "Have you been following up on other suspects?"

Crossing his arms, the overweight detective frowned. "And what other suspects would that be, Agent Donovan?"

James held up the plastic bag. "I have possible evidence from Katherine McKray's flat indicating at least two people were inside."

Tenner's bushy eyebrows knitted. "I thought we gave her place a pretty good going-over."

They had, and James resisted the urge to shake him for it. "These two cups were in the dishwasher and Ms. McKray insists she didn't use them. Did you or your men happen to?"

"No."

"Then someone else was in her apartment long enough to enjoy a cup of coffee. I suspect her friend Denise Womack had a guest over, although she denied it. Perhaps you'd better have her fingerprinted to check against these cups."

"We know how to do our job here, Agent," Tenner said as he reached for the bag.

James removed a pen from an inside jacket pocket. "Unfortunately, you'll find Ms. McKray's prints on them, and the fellow at the front who's keeping my gun until I leave. Will you please keep me informed at this number?" He started to scratch on a scrap piece of paper on the desk, but Tenner interrupted him.

"Flagiron Hotel, room twelve forty-five." The man grinned widely, showing coffee-stained teeth. "Like I said, we know how to do our job, Agent."

Kat set the picture of her father on the bookshelf and rubbed her thumb over his face until tears blurred her focus. She sniffed hard and went back to her task of restoring order to the living room. Her body throbbed from exhaustion and some other distant ache that worsened when she thought of Agent James Donovan.

She ought to be in bed, regaining her strength in preparation for the week ahead, which, unless someone stepped forward and confessed to the crime, promised to deteriorate even further. But if she kept her hands busy, she wouldn't dwell on the upheaval in her life. The phone rang a dozen times, and each time she was tempted to answer it, in case James was calling. But she resisted and allowed it to roll over to her answering machine.

Several reporters called. Andy Wharton left a message saying he hoped she'd be back to work soon—how were they going to host the open house next week without her? Despite her predicament, Kat felt anxious about the success of Jellico's annual open house—old habits and loyalties, however misplaced, were hard to break.

Guy also called, to let Kat know he'd received her message that she'd received his message. Kat bounced a cushion off the phone as he talked. Dammit, the little bastard always had to have the last word.

Denise called twice, and Kat almost picked up to talk to her friend, but she remembered James's earlier warning about not discussing the coffee cups until he had done a background check. And although Denise sounded much too concerned for Kat's welfare to be remotely involved in this mess, she heeded his warning and made a mental note to call her tomorrow.

Heaving a sigh, she straightened her stiff back and surveyed her progress. Actually, things were looking pretty good—she'd weeded out three bags of garbage as she sifted through magazines, books, and newspapers. A silver lining in every cloud, she mused, no matter how black.

She moved a CD rack from which her music had been dumped, and something shiny caught her eye. Intrigued, Kat picked it up and turned it over, then gasped.

The stolen compass. Her heart thudded against her ribs. How on earth had it gotten here? Then she jumped back and let it fall onto an area rug. Her prints were all over it now. She backed away from it, wrapping her arms around herself, and glancing around wildly. If someone had taken her clothing and badge, they could just as easily have planted the compass. Then her stomach turned over. Had the police found other items stolen from the gallery hidden in her apartment?

She had to get out—the naked walls were unfriendly and closing in around her, the haphazard stacks of debris a reminder of the violence with which she was being targeted. But why?

Kat stumbled into her bedroom and jammed on her glasses. The bulb in her lamp flickered, then went out, plunging the room into darkness. She felt her way into the bathroom and pawed the wall for the light switch. The tiny room's illumination cast enough glow into the bedroom for Kat to scrounge up a warm coat, gloves, and shoes. Her feet had carried her out to the lamplit sidewalk before the cold breeze slowed her down.

Music from Sissy's café down the street drifted out to mingle with the sounds of passing cars and clumps of pedestrians hurrying to their destinations. A raggedy young man sitting on the stoop of the four-story building across the street tipped his hat at her and took a quick drag on a joint. Kat eyed him suspiciously, her pulse leaping. Everyone—everything—looked more sinister today than yesterday. Somewhere in the city, possibly within her circle of acquaintances, lurked a person who didn't mind that she was about to be indicted for a crime she didn't commit.

She didn't have a vehicle, and even if she did, where would she go? Kat glanced about frantically for a direction that seemed right . . . east? . . . north? A southbound bus belched its way up the street and lurched to a stop at the corner several yards away. If she ran, she could make it . . . but she stood frozen with indecision.

Miserable, Kat mentally scanned her list of friends and acquaintances—lots of nice people, but not many she would burden with her scandalous company at the moment. And while Denise would take her with open arms, Kat wasn't eager for the barrage of questions she knew she'd be subjected to. Andy? Guy would probably fire him if Andy let her stay at his place.

Dammit, as much as she hated to admit it—she needed James . . . no, she *wanted* James. She wanted his big, comforting presence, his pleasing velvety accent, his gently rolling conversation. His hotel was only a few blocks away, normally safe walking distance night or day in the part of town she lived in, but thoroughly spooked, Kat walked to the deserted corner and hailed a taxi under the glare of the streetlight.

Even if he weren't in his room, she'd be satisfied to sit in a busy lobby just for the comfort of a crowd. In fact, she'd book a room for herself until she could get the locks changed on her door. Feeling much better, she laid her head back and closed her eyes for a few seconds, willing her body to slow down. But unrelenting waves of fear, disbelief, and anger pumped a steady stream of adrenaline through her body. Her heart still pounded erratically as she walked through the grand entrance of the Flagiron Hotel.

She stood in line for ten minutes behind camera-laden visitors with restless children, then stepped up to the smiling woman behind the desk. "I'd like a room, please."

"Hiding out?" a familiar British voice asked behind her.

Kat spun to see James standing with his lips pressed together, his eyes questioning. His cheeks were wind-flushed—he'd apparently just returned. "Not hiding. I . . . I don't feel safe at my apartment. I decided to have the locks changed."

"Good idea." He addressed the clerk with a cajoling smile as he removed black driving gloves. "Is a room available next to twelve forty-five?"

The woman melted at the sound of his voice, then

straightened, her fingers flying over her keyboard. "Yes, sir—twelve forty-seven."

"Good. Please quarter Ms. McKray there."

Two days ago she would have shredded a man who presumed to make such a decision for her. But Kat didn't object to the arrangement, even though the prospect of sleeping in proximity to James was comforting and unsettling at the same time.

He took her key while she signed for the room. "Where is your luggage?"

Now she really felt silly. "I guess I left in a hurry."

His black brows knitted. "Did something happen?"

Kat thought of the valuable gold compass lying on the rug in her living room. "Yes."

He reached for her arm. "Are you all right?"

She nodded, touched by his concern. "Fine—but I found something the police apparently missed while mine-sweeping my apartment."

James's frown deepened and he glanced around. "Let's go upstairs where we can talk—I uncovered a few things the police overlooked myself."

He hovered close as they waited for an elevator, then waved her inside the glass enclosure. Kat shuffled in on elastic legs and kept her back turned to the view. She had never minded heights, but today her reflexes seemed hypersensitive, and spiraling toward the twelfth floor made her light-headed. The feel of James's hands on her waist sent her body into a further state of chaos.

"We might have taken the stairs," he murmured against her hair, "but I'd rather you conserve your energy for other pursuits." His low chuckle told her he was teasing, trying to lighten the mood, and she warmed to his bantering, suddenly glad she'd come.

He opened her door and flicked on a light before

stepping aside for her to enter. Dressed in pleasing golds and soothing yellows, her room was luxurious with overstuffed furnishings and rugs thick enough to trip up a tired person's feet. Just the sight of the waist-high queen-size bed reminded her how many hours she'd been running on empty. She glanced at her watch. Almost eleven, but she was still too keyed up to rest. James retrieved two glasses from the top of a pale wood dresser, then disappeared into the bathroom.

Kat sank into one of the two armchairs, then kicked off her shoes and dragged her feet to the single large ottoman that serviced both chairs. Feeling oddly out-of-body, she stared into space, as if she were observing someone else experiencing all the craziness of the last day. She clawed her hair back from her temples, digging her fingernails into her scalp, triggering the kind of cleansing pain that relieves stress. A little.

The water splashed on and off. A few seconds later, James emerged to hand her a cool glass, then sat in the chair opposite hers. The lighting in the room was more decorative than utilitarian, lending a golden intimacy to the room. Which, she decided, was what the designers had intended, considering the activities that had most likely taken place hundreds of times in this room.

With shaking hands, she drained the glass, then laid her head back.

"You're exhausted," he said quietly.

She affirmed his observation with a half murmur, half grunt. "But not sleepy." She wondered if her eyes were as bugged out as they felt. "I found the gold compass that was stolen from the gallery while I was cleaning up."

He pursed his lips, and she wondered what was going on behind those shrouded dark eyes. "And you have no idea how it got there."

His statement was calm, but her defenses rallied nonetheless. "Well, obviously someone put it there, but it wasn't me."

Sighing, he steepled his hands. "In addition to the clothing, the police found one of the missing rings during their search."

Kat closed her eyes, summoning strength. "Who could be doing this to me?"

"I have a theory, but you won't want to hear it."

She opened her eyes and lifted her head. "What is it?"

"Your friend Denise has more secrets than I suspected."

Swallowing hard, Kat gripped the empty glass. "Like what?"

"Like a record for repeated petty thefts."

Her stomach churned. "When?"

"The most recent one was twelve years ago. Shoplifting clothes and jewelry."

Kat did the arithmetic in her head. "She would have been in college." She frowned. "I'm disappointed, but that was a long time ago."

James drummed his long, tapered fingers together. "There's more. Thirty thousand dollars was deposited in her checking account this morning."

Her stomach heaved and her lips parted. "Denise? Where on earth . . . do you think she could have stolen the letter and sold it?"

"It's quite possible," he said, his tone grave. "Would she have such contacts?"

Kat glanced around the room, her mind racing, trying to recall conversations, people, places. "The Chinese have a corner on the import-export trade on the West Coast, so naturally they also control the black market."

She pressed her lips together, then looked back at James. "Denise hangs out in Chinatown—she likes Asian men."

His black eyebrows rose a fraction. "Ah. And as a model, I suspect she has access to wigs and such."

Tears pricked her eyes as she nodded. *Not Denise.*

Leaning toward the ottoman, he captured her stockinged feet in his hands and fingered the delicate bones of her ankles. "Kat, I'm sure this is hurtful to you, but it's good news—at the very least it's enough evidence to instill doubt in the minds of the grand jury."

She shook her head, disbelief coursing through her. "I would have to hear it from her own mouth."

"Shhhh," he whispered, stroking the tops of her feet. "Things will look better in the morning, Pussy-Kat. I'm glad you decided to come here—I'll feel better knowing you're nearby." He nodded to a narrow door beside the dresser and smiled, dimples carved deep in his cheeks. "And look—our rooms adjoin in the event you find yourself in need of"—he cleared his throat—"an alibi."

His hands sent shivers up her legs, straight to the core of her desire. Her toes curled involuntarily, and her eyelids floated down. It would be soooo easy to let herself be swept away for the night, to lie beneath him and revel in the coming together of their bodies. He wanted her, and she wanted him. Their kisses were so sizzling, their coupling was bound to be mind-blowing. Why not? After all, he'd be leaving soon.

A sharp pain pierced her chest even as his hands worked magic. He'd be leaving soon. And taking with him the fleeting memory of another conquest. She, on the other hand, would be left with the idealized perception of a hero no other man could live up to.

Years ago she'd gotten through that hormone-crazed period where she believed physical love was synonymous with spiritual love. Now she was looking for someone to share the simple pleasures of life, someone who wanted a family and a measure of the American dream she'd observed on television.

She opened her eyes and absorbed James's image: gorgeous, sexy beyond belief, charming . . . and completely untouchable. She deserved more than a casual affair, and she wasn't about to settle.

He moved his ministrations to her calves, kneading her flesh through the thin knit of her leggings.

Kat swallowed. Not even if he made her feel weak with longing.

His fingers traced circles over her knees, then moved higher to caress her thighs.

Her breath caught in her chest, and her gaze locked with his. Not even if he made her forget her surroundings.

He leaned forward and inched his hand beneath the tail of her shirt, grazing the sensitive mound between her thighs.

Kat's knees came up instinctively. Not even if he made her forget her name.

She opened her mouth to protest before she lost the ability to speak, but his mouth closed over hers, stealing the words from her throat. This kiss held no tenderness, simply hard passion as he gathered her in his arms, pulled her forward onto the ottoman, and cradled her between his knees.

His tongue wrought havoc on hers, teasing, battling, conquering. She shuddered, her nipples beading and scalding wetness warming her thighs. Her mind spun, racing to transmit a desperate message, a memory of what she'd been thinking the second before his lips touched hers. She had the faint feeling that the notion had been an important one, but it eluded her.

James felt a strange, scary feeling erupt as he held Kat against him and delved into the sweet recesses of her mouth. Unidentifiable, the emotion pressing against his chest could best be compared to the time he had parachuted directly into a guerrilla camp in South America. And he had the distinct impression that he would not be able to shoot himself out of this situation.

He lifted his head and studied her blue eyes, smoky with passion. Inhaling sharply, he released her and stood in one motion, albeit unsteadily. He'd crossed the room, opened the door, and taken one step into the hallway before he realized he owed her some token of an explanation. Turning, he took one look at her kiss-softened mouth and forgot whatever clever quip he'd intended to deliver.

An indistinct good-night was the best he could manage, then he pulled the door shut and escaped into his own room.

EIGHT

Kat awoke before dawn, still achy and fatigued from the restless night. The shadow of her friend's possible betrayal had weighed heavily on her mind, and James's abrupt departure had only heightened the prickly, coming-out-of-her-skin feeling. She'd lain awake and stared at the digital clock radio, listening to the couple in the next room make wall-thumping, hair-raising love until the wee hours of the morning.

And now it appeared from the frantic sounds coming from the other side of the wall, they were also early risers—if indeed they had ever closed their eyes.

She lay still, watching the first fingers of light caress the ceiling, and tried not to think about the flimsy door that stood between James's room and hers.

Tried not to think about the passions he'd torched in her last night before ruthlessly tearing out of their embrace and leaving her smoldering with a lukewarm goodnight.

Tried not to think about the fact that she'd slept in the buff, half because she didn't have a gown, half because she had a virginal yearning for him to crash through the connecting door and claim her with as few delays as possible.

Her logical side told her to be eternally grateful for whatever had prompted his timely exit—she had been disappointed before by the change in a man's demeanor on the "morning after." Hindsight had taught her the zenith of a man's affection crested just before the first night of sex, then moved into a gradual but steady state of decline shortly thereafter. Currently, she needed James's friendship and expertise more than she needed his carnal attention.

The woman's muffled moans of "more, more, more" floated through the wall. Kat clamped the extra pillow on her face and pressed the ends over her ears. Okay, at the moment, she needed his carnal attention more, but the feeling would abate with the harsh reality of daylight . . . she hoped.

By the time the couple had spent themselves, the clock read ten minutes before six and Kat felt like she needed a cigarette. That brought her father's humidor to mind, and she breathed a prayer of thanks as she swung her feet to the floor that James had been able to remove it. She hadn't thought to ask him where he'd stashed it, but she assumed it was in his car or in his hotel room. Kat sighed—all roads led back to his room.

She pulled herself to her feet and stumbled to the shower, glad for the mind-clearing blast of water. Mixed feelings about the case pressed upon her . . . relief that she was no longer the only suspect, along with anguish that her best friend had been fingered. Had she simply done it for the money? The idea that Denise would frame her still flabbergasted Kat, but she couldn't deny that the evidence was convincing.

But then again, the evidence against herself had been convincing too.

Her mind strayed as her hands traveled over her lathered shoulders, arms, and breasts. She could see her naked image through the frosty shower door reflected back in the mirror over the vanity. She couldn't resist wondering if James would have been pleased. Her curves were generous, and her waist trim—her body wasn't exactly coin-bouncing firm, but not too shabby, either, she decided as the water beaded on her oiled skin. A warm flush climbed her neck when she thought of James's admiring glances the first night he'd come to her apartment door. So much had changed since then.

At least in *her* mind. *And heart*, she admitted with a resigned sigh.

So she was hung up on him, so what? He would pass on and so would her feelings and she would live through it, she decided as she turned off the faucet. She wrapped a large towel around her body and a smaller one around her hair, turban-style.

Well, at least she'd had the good sense not to sleep with him. Kat ignored the voice that questioned how far she would've gone if he hadn't pulled back.

She switched on the morning news for noise, tensing through the thirty-second update on the break-in of the gallery. "The police have charged Katherine McKray, a longtime employee, with stealing the love letter that King George III wrote to a mistress over two hundred years ago."

"*Allegedly* wrote," Kat corrected the announcer. "And I didn't take the letter." She cursed and hoped that news of her innocence would garner the same amount of coverage. At least they hadn't shown her picture.

With one leg propped on the unmade bed, she

massaged the hotel's aloe lotion into her skin and thought of James sleeping in the next room. He seemed so omnipotent, it was hard to imagine his requiring something as pedestrian as sleep. Did he lie naked, sprawled over the entire bed with nonchalance, or fully dressed on the edge with his gun at his waist? Chill bumps zipped over her glowing skin and she frowned at the connecting door. A knock upon it startled her so badly she dropped the small bottle, bouncing it across the rug.

"Kat?" James asked softly, then knocked again. "Are you awake?"

Re-tucking the corner of her towel under her arm self-consciously, she stepped toward the door. "Yes, James, I'm awake."

"May I come in?"

She looked around the room frantically, searching for the shirt she'd worn yesterday. "Um, just a minute, I'm not decent."

His throaty laughter rumbled through the inch of wood. "I sincerely doubt that, Pussy-Kat."

Oh, that voice was going to be the end of her. Her pulse kicked up instantly, dewing her hairline as she dropped the towel and pulled her day-old clothes from the back of a chair and onto her body. She winced down at her baggy-kneed leggings. Barefoot and braless, she unlocked the door and swung it open.

The door pulled with it the scent of his grooming, tickling her nose with strong mannish aromas. James filled the doorway, wearing perfectly creased navy slacks and a crisp taupe-colored long-sleeved shirt. The top two buttons were undone, revealing a slice of a sparkling white T-shirt which she guessed had also been pressed within an inch of its life. "Do you travel with a personal valet?" she asked, peering around him.

He smiled, a breathtaking gesture. "I'm glad to see your sense of humor has recovered."

Not a word about what had nearly transpired between them last night, proof positive of its insignificance—to him. "I'm almost a free woman," she said lightly. "I need to call Val and let him know where I am, plus the fact that the police have a new suspect."

"*Will* have a new suspect after we talk with Detective Tenner and the district attorney. I left a message for Tenner that we'd see him this morning, and your attorney will need to accompany us." He stopped and angled his head slightly. "Perhaps you can arrange to take the polygraph while we're there."

Kat's heart tripped and she swallowed. "Do you think that will still be necessary?" As James studied her face, she fought to keep the fear from her eyes by attempting a small shrug.

James sensed her trepidation. Was she hiding something or simply nervous at the prospect of taking the test? "That will be up to you and your attorney," he said in a low tone.

She brushed aside the topic with a cheerful smile, noticeably forced. "Let me dry my hair, then I'll need to stop by the apartment for clothes and toiletries."

He nodded, relenting. Perhaps he was mistaking awkwardness over their encounter last night for guilt. And he certainly didn't want to dredge up *that* unsettling subject. "I'll order breakfast—what would you like?"

She headed back toward the bathroom and released her hair from the towel with a flick of her wrist. It tumbled around her shoulders in thick, separated locks. "A bagel sounds great," she said, "or maybe some hot cereal. And coffee."

James stood rooted to the spot as she picked up a pink comb, squinted into the vanity mirror, and leaned forward to part her hair. For a few seconds, the wet, dark carpet of mane concealed her face, then she swept the heavy strands back over her ears carefully with the comb. It struck him as infinitely intimate, watching her fuss with her hair, and quite possibly the most innocently erotic scene he'd ever witnessed.

From a tiny tube she squeezed a clear substance into her palm, rubbed her hands together, then massaged the shiny stuff from her scalp to the ends. Silhouetted by the glaring overhead light and with her arms lifted high, it was suddenly quite apparent that beneath the rumpled white shirt, she wore no bra. The dusky outline of her nipples riveted him. James felt his manhood twitch in warning, then surge.

In Europe, it was common to see bare-breasted women—on public beaches, in advertisements—so he, like most traveled Englishmen, had seen a fair amount of comely busts in somewhat casual settings. In the past, he'd found the puritan practice of American women binding and covering their God-given gifts to be, in turn, annoying and stimulating. And at the moment, the glimpse of taboo flesh was uncomfortably stimulating.

Kat's gaze cut to his in the mirror. "The stronger, the better."

James shook his head slightly in confusion, willing his libido to heel. "Pardon?"

"The coffee," she said, unhooking a hair dryer from a wall holder. "The stronger, the better."

"Right," he said, straightening. "Strong coffee coming up."

She flicked a switch, eliciting the whine of the hair dryer, blowing her lustrous hair back from her face like some exotic model photo shoot. He turned and retreated into his room, chastising himself for allowing her to reduce him to a gawking schoolboy, when a stiff breeze would've had him chafing in his drawers.

He dialed room service and ordered enough food for both of them. Glancing at the open connecting door, he resisted the urge to watch Kat complete her toilette and instead drew aside the curtains in his room to admire the spectacular twelfth-story view.

San Francisco was a picturesque city, with hundreds of old Victorian row houses snuggled together in the hills, utilizing every square foot of scarce and expensive land. Their ice-cream colors and dark roofs with identical pitches reminded him of the patchwork quilt that used to cover the foot of his mother's bed. She'd called the pattern "tumbling blocks," although he had no idea how he remembered such an obscure detail from a life lived twenty-five years ago.

Diabetes had snatched her from them when he was not quite a full-grown man, and his father had succumbed less than a year later, of a broken heart, James was convinced. His older sister had been dating the man she'd eventually married, so for the most part, James had been left to his own devices.

Later, his superiors and co-agents at British Intelligence had become his family, although he acknowledged that, out of necessity, everyone conducted themselves more like distant relatives. In the ensuing years, he'd grown fond of his own company . . . but suddenly he felt a swell of reverence for that elusive connection to another person, the bond which had crossed ethereal boundaries for his parents.

Why these bittersweet domestic memories were descending on him now, he couldn't fathom. He peered back over his shoulder and bit the inside of his cheek—maybe his mood had something to do with Katherine McKray and the feelings she had dislodged within him. As if on cue, the muffled sound of her honeyed voice, half humming, half singing, invaded his room above the static noise of the hair dryer. The song was indistinguishable, but her tone sounded sweet and melancholy. And beckoning.

He abandoned his station at the window and, against his will, took three strides toward her room before a knock on his door pulled him up short.

"Room service," a Spanish accent called through the door.

Grateful for the distraction, James claimed the food and tipped the man, then set the covered tray on an impractical looking writing desk. He stepped to the doorway to summon Kat, and leaned against the door frame, arms crossed, to watch her. Once again he was struck by her natural beauty as she finished drying her dark hair and sang to herself, apparently oblivious to being heard. She glanced up and stopped, mid-note, then blushed furiously and switched off the dryer.

"Very nice," he said, grinning.

"I didn't realize you could hear me."

"I assure you, I found it delightful. Breakfast has arrived."

She plucked her glasses from the vanity and slid them on, then preceded him into his room, her gaze pivoting from one side to the other. "Wow, I'll bet it's neater in here now than when you checked in."

He shrugged, feeling a bit sheepish. "I'm trained not to leave a trail—I guess old habits die hard."

A pang of disappointment cut through Kat's chest. "So," she said lightly, lifting the silver lid from the tray, "when you leave, no one will even know you've been here, is that what you're saying?"

He was quiet for so long, she glanced up to find his head angled toward her. "Are you saying you will miss me, Pussy-Kat?" His voice was husky and colored with surprise.

She dropped the lid and lifted her chin. "I said no such thing."

His mouth twisted in an infuriating smile, then he wagged his finger at her and stepped closer. "Ah-ah, thou doth protest too much."

She swallowed, her gaze darting around the room. "You're putting words in my mouth."

"Then allow me to occupy it elsewhere," he murmured, pulling her into his arms.

Her heart cartwheeled as he dipped his head with calculating slowness and captured her lips with his. The desire she'd smothered all morning, hoping to extinguish, rose like a phoenix out of the flames. All the reasons to avoid this man who'd become much too important to her, much too quickly, were incinerated as his mouth moved against hers. With his tongue, he coaxed her mouth open, then ravaged the inside ruthlessly, stealing, commanding, demanding.

Her glasses became too fogged to see clearly—surely that was why everything seemed blurry?—but her other senses roared to life. He moved his warm hands beneath her shirt to span her back and waist, and Kat instantly felt her nipples bead. She moaned into his mouth and he shuddered against her, fueling her passion higher. He massaged her back in small circles, tracing her spine, lazily working his way up and around to caress the sides of her quivering rib cage. When the urgency of his kiss intensified, she rolled her shoulders and inhaled sharply, poised for the feel of his hands on her breasts. But just when his thumbs grazed the underside of her bosom, he lifted his head and slowly straightened, then dropped his hands away from her.

Confusion washed over Kat. She wet her lips carefully, then asked in a deadly calm voice, "Is this where you mumble good night and make a hasty retreat, Agent Donovan?"

He stared down at her with a clouded expression. "Kat, you're vulnerable right now. I don't wish to take advantage—"

"In case you hadn't noticed, James, I'm all grown up." She pressed her lips together hard. "Able to make my own decisions, and live with the consequences."

He pulled her closer to him, and rested his forehead against hers. "And you want this as much as I do, Pussy-Kat?"

In answer, she took one step back, looked him directly in the eye, and began to unbutton her shirt.

As if spellbound, his gaze dropped to her fingers. With outward control that belied her quaking insides, Kat divorced the white buttons from their buttonholes, never taking her eyes off James's face. When she'd reached the bottom, she paused, allowing the shirt to reveal an inch-wide strip of her cleavage and stomach. His lips parted, his undivided attention on her covered breasts.

Ever so slowly, she peeled the fabric back, feeling her nipples contract as soon as the cool air of the room enveloped them. Passion glazed his eyes, gratifying her. She thrust her breasts forward in a slow-moving shrug out of her shirt. The whoosh of the cotton garment falling to the rug sounded like a lead weight dropping in the silence of the room.

"Kat," he breathed, standing statue-still. "You are magnificent."

A thrill raced through her body. "So touch me," she whispered.

"I thought you'd never ask." He bent and swept her into his arms, then laid her gently on his bed. She removed her glasses and folded them safely on the nightstand. He stood and kicked off his shoes, then shed his shirt and undershirt, tossing them carelessly onto an armchair.

Heat and moisture pooled between her legs at the sight of his naked torso—broad, muscled shoulders, lightly haired chest, with dark, flat nipples indented in firm flesh. He lowered himself beside her, supported on one elbow while his hungry gaze swept over her bared breasts. Lifting his free hand, his fingers hovered over a budded nipple almost reverently before descending for a soft squeeze that elicited a groan from both of them. Sexual energy raced through her body, triggering chills in one place, muscle contraction in another. He kneaded her breasts and reclaimed her mouth, his breathing as frantic as hers.

Kat arched toward him, rolling on her side to face him and press her breasts against his chest, hot skin on hot skin. He interrupted their kiss long enough to whisper, "I have to taste you, Pussy-Kat," then lowered his head to lave her nipple thoroughly. He licked, nipped, and drew as much of her breast into his greedy mouth as possible, devouring her. And when she thought she would go insane from the waves of desire flooding her body, he shifted his attention to her other breast and started over.

Anxious to touch every inch of his flesh, Kat ran her finger around his waistband, stumbling over various tabs and buttons, at last revealing white boxer shorts and his straining shaft. James paused from his ministrations just long enough to groan with satisfaction when her fingers closed around him.

Driven by the rhythm of his mouth on her skin, she stroked him, drawing wetness that oozed down over her fingers. His hand snaked down to palm her stomach, then pushed the flimsy leggings over her hips and plunged his hand into her drenched nest. Hot splinters of desire bolted through her and she convulsed around his probing fingers, gasping. With feet and legs, they skimmed off each other's remaining clothes, at last lying on their sides fully naked against each other, mouth to mouth, hand to hand, sex to sex.

Kat wondered if her face held the same expression of desire and blatant need as James's. His black eyes were hooded with passion, his smooth cheeks and forehead covered with a fine sheen of perspiration. His lips parted slightly, as if he wanted to say something.

"James?" she whispered. "Is something wrong?"

An unidentifiable emotion flitted across his face, then it was gone just as quickly. His mouth pulled back to reveal both dimples as he rolled her beneath him. "No, Pussy-Kat, everything seems to be in top working order." With his knee, he urged her to open to him, and she obliged almost involuntarily, readying herself for his swift entry. But he took his time, rubbing his hard staff against her slick folds, circling the sensitive nub of her desire with mind-blowing accuracy. A slow hum of pressure began building low inside her, like a swarm of tiny, vibrating bees. Then with a groan of raw passion, he thrust inside her.

At the feel of him burrowing deep, Kat gasped and drew up her knees, squeezing hard, arching her pebbled breasts against the solid wall of his chest. He resumed the pleasure he'd set in motion between her thighs by massaging her with his thumb in time to his long, unhurried strokes. With soft, raspy words of encouragement in her ear, he coaxed her mounting orgasm to the surface until she succumbed to the white-hot flash of release, crying out in abandon and digging her fingers deep into the flesh of his back as he rode through the waves with her.

As Kat trembled around him, James felt dangerously close to losing control, and not of his body. In the many times he'd lain with women and shared carnal pleasures, he'd always managed to distance himself from the intimacy by concentrating on the act itself instead of the person. Only now, he felt overwhelmed by Kat's essence . . . of her beneath him, all around him, her smells, her cries, her hands, her mouth. . . . His muscles bunched, readying him for the terrific explosion building in his loins. He plunged inside her silken depths one last time and shuddered his release over and over as sheets of pleasure-pain coursed through his body.

He slumped over her, smoothed back her hair and kissed her face around the smiles, nuzzling her neck and sharing low growls as their bodies pulsed with latent contractions. He'd suspected the minute he set his gaze upon her that she would be a luxurious lover. James sighed in satisfaction—at least his instincts in that department were still reliable.

It was only after he rolled to her side, gulping air to slow his pounding pulse that a thunderbolt of realization struck in horrific clarity—he'd actually gasped her name in the throes of his ecstasy.

Kat . . . Kat . . . my Pussy-Kat. Floored by his own lapse, and the possible implication to his emotional well-being, James lay stock-still.

"James?" Leaned up on one elbow, Kat tucked a strand of dark hair behind her ear and stared down at him. "You look like you have regrets."

His mind spinning with revelation, he glanced up into her clear blue eyes and felt like a condemned man. But if he'd learned anything in the last twenty years, he'd learned not to allow the opponent to see the chink in his armor. Act normal, as if his world hadn't just turned bottom side up. So he conjured up a charming smile and gave her a wicked wink. "Just one regret, Pussy-Kat—that we wasted so much time last night sleeping."

Her laughter filled the room, then she left the bed and walked toward the abandoned breakfast tray. "I'm starved." She lifted the lid and snatched a strawberry.

"Then let's eat," James suggested cheerfully, glad she seemed at ease with her superbly curved body. Then he shifted as his erection began a slow climb—he only wished he could be so nonchalant about her rounded hips and heavy breasts.

"I'll be right back," Kat said, then headed toward his bathroom with a wry smile. "I need to clean up your trail."

James watched her walk away and wondered how she had managed to worm her way into his well-guarded heart in only a couple of days. But even more important, how the devil was he going to evict her from the premises?

NINE

As James delivered his theory in the cramped interrogation room, Kat wondered if the idea of Denise Womack pulling off the heist sounded as ludicrous to everyone else as it did to her. And on top of her other concerns, she found it difficult to keep her eyes off him while he was talking. Since they'd left the hotel, she'd tried not to analyze the emotional fallout of their deed, yet stiff muscles had kept the memory of their energetic lovemaking close at hand.

Shifting uncomfortably in the metal chair, she flicked her gaze to Valmer Getty as James wrapped up with the information Kat had told him about Denise's penchant for Asian lovers. Dressed in outdated, casual clothes, her attorney sat forward on his seat, nodding his head non-stop in support throughout the recitation.

The assistant district attorney, a middle-aged woman of Hispanic descent, scribbled notes on a pad with an expensive pen. She looked as though she had been on her way to church when summoned to the station. So far, she hadn't asked a single question.

"So, Agent Donovan." Detective Tenner rose slowly to assume a wide-legged, authoritative stance—incongruous since his fly was down. "How did you discover the Womack woman had that sum of money deposited in her account?"

James lifted his shoulders in a casual shrug. "I have my sources—it was a matter of a simple phone call."

Kat nearly smiled at his nonchalance, but Tenner obviously didn't like James having the jump on him. His eyes narrowed. "I thought someone said you were retired."

"I am," James affirmed, then offered an amiable smile. "Detective, someone is trying to frame Ms. McKray, and in doing so, is endeavoring to trick you. We can get to the root of this matter if we work together."

"He's right, Tenner," Valmer chimed in, then extended a sweeping, empathetic smile to the detective and to the D.A. "Plus I'm sure neither your department nor Ms. Pena's needs a lawsuit from my client if she's indicted and tried when the police have substantial evidence that someone else might have perpetrated the crime." Kat felt a surge of appreciation toward Val. And a surge of something stronger toward James.

Ms. Pena pursed her lips, then capped her pen and stood. "Go check it out, Detective. Judge Tyler won't appreciate being disturbed on Sunday morning, but I'll handle the search warrant."

Tenner gave a curt nod of resignation, then grimaced at James. "I suppose you want to go with me, Secret Agent Man?"

James nodded. "And I think it would be beneficial if Ms. McKray went along as well—after all, she knows the woman better than anyone else."

Everyone turned their gaze upon her. She wanted to decline, but Val had instructed her not to talk. Sitting there in silence, she hoped Tenner would object.

The detective frowned sourly in her direction, then withdrew a nugget of five-cent bubble gum from his pocket and unwrapped it. He noticed his open zipper and righted himself without turning away. "We got about an hour to kill, Ms. McKray. What say we give our polygrapher a call?"

Kat's heart jumped to her throat. "Now?"

Ms. Pena nodded in agreement, then addressed Val. "My office is not interested in prosecuting the wrong person, Counselor. Give me enough proof, and we'll drop the charges."

Valmer smiled magnanimously. "Call your technician—my client has nothing to hide."

Kat felt James's gaze upon her, but she was too busy trying to look innocent to acknowledge him.

On the other side of a two-way mirror, James sat with Kat's attorney and watched as she was led to a dingy upholstered chair, then connected to several monitors. Her face looked pinched, and her skin pale. He had a bad feeling about the test, primarily due to the fact that Kat herself had seemed less than enthusiastic each time the polygraph had been mentioned. Still, if she was innocent—and he believed her to be—then the results could help clear her name.

The polygraph machine hummed to life, its avenging needles sliding across the page in a carefree scribble. Kat's eyes widened and she looked terrified.

Val clucked. "Poor dear is nervous."

For her sake, James hoped apprehension was the only cause of her anxiety.

"Relax, Ms. McKray," the spectacled technician said woodenly. "I'll ask you a series of questions and you are to respond yes or no, is that clear?"

"Yes," she said, causing the needles to shimmy about a quarter inch, then level out.

"Is your name Katherine McKray?"

"Yes."

"Do you live at One Twenty-four Tangled Vine?"

"Yes."

"Is your birthday March third?"

"No."

"Have you ever been employed by Jellico's Gallery and Museum?"

"Yes."

James kept his eye on the polygraph, gratified that she seemed to be relaxing. She answered more mundane questions, then the man asked, "Did you steal the item known as the King George letter?"

"No."

"Were you born in the state of California?"

"Yes."

"Have you ever stolen an item from the gallery known as Jellico's?"

"No."

James watched the needles and pressed his lips together at their movement. The man progressed through a series of about six-dozen questions, of which twenty or so concerned the burglary. The dread in the pit of his stomach grew as the questions, reworded in every possible combination, became more pointed. Kat was visibly relieved when the man announced the test was over.

"How soon will they have a reading?" James asked Valmer, who had remained silent during the exam.

"They should call me with an opinion later this afternoon," the man replied, noticeably distracted. "I'll notify Kat immediately."

"Will she be allowed to take the test again?" James asked, looking the man directly in the eye.

Valmer stared, then sighed and nodded curtly. "I have to leave. Tell Katherine I'll be in touch."

She appeared a few moments later, and James gave her Val's message. "How did it go?" he asked, studying her face.

Fanning herself, she attempted a laugh. "I was so nervous, I could barely concentrate. I probably failed the damn thing."

James reached out with his finger and tipped her chin until her gaze met his. "This lovely face couldn't belong to a liar," he said softly.

Her shaky smile was not reassuring.

"I'm not so sure about this," Kat murmured to James.

"If you're with us, she may be more inclined to talk," he said as they followed Tenner to Denise's apartment door.

She inhaled deeply and nodded. "Denise is a late riser, especially on the weekends," she offered nervously when Detective Tenner knocked for the third time. It was after eleven o'clock and her stomach churned at the prospect of the impending conversation. For an instant, she hoped her friend was off having breakfast with her mystery man. Yet even though she didn't want to believe the worst, she had to concede that Denise did owe her the truth.

The truth. Kat nearly laughed aloud. She was a fine one to talk, after losing track of the fibs she'd told during the polygraph. Her only hope now was that someone else would be fingered for the crime. While she didn't relish the idea of visiting her best friend in jail, at the moment it ranked slightly higher than the prospect of returning there herself.

Denise was knotting the sash on her silk robe when she opened the door. Her friend smoothed a thin hand over her sleep-tousled hair, looked straight past Tenner brandishing a shiny ID badge, and narrowed on Kat, who lagged behind everyone else in the hall.

"Kat? Is everything okay? What's going on?"

Kat opened her mouth, hoping some kind of reasonable, non-accusatory explanation would emerge. But Tenner cut in, extending his arm against the door, as if he were afraid she would deny them access. "Ms. Womack, I need to ask you some more questions about the night of the break-in at Jellico's Gallery."

The woman's delicate eyebrows furrowed, then she shrugged. "Sure. Come on in."

Kat hung back, watching as James allowed Officers Campbell and Raines to precede him. When he waved her forward, she shook her head. "I still don't buy it, James."

He nodded sympathetically. "Then perhaps your friend will recall a detail that will lead us in the right direction."

She brightened a little, then entered the messy living area of the apartment. If she hadn't known better, she would have sworn that Tenner's men had already searched the place. But Denise was not particular when it came to orderliness.

The rotund detective glanced around, then said, "Be advised, Ms. Womack, we have a search warrant for your apartment, and you may be considered a suspect in the burglary. Would you like to call an attorney?"

Kat's stomach rolled as Denise blanched. "Excuse me?" Wheeling toward Kat, Denise's eyes bulged. "Kat, what the hell is going on?"

"Denise—" Kat began, but Tenner cut her off.

"Ms. Womack do you waive the right to have an attorney present?"

Her friend flushed red and looked him up and down, glaring. "I didn't have anything to do with the break-in, so why would I need an attorney?"

"So you do waive your right?" Tenner pressed.

Denise gestured impatiently. "Yeah, yeah, already. Get to the point."

"Okay," Tenner said smoothly. "Would you mind telling us about the thirty thousand dollars that appeared in your bank account yesterday?"

Denise crossed her arms over her chest in a protective gesture. "How," she squeaked, "did you get access to my financial records?"

"Just answer the question, miss," Tenner barked.

Her gaze cut to Kat, who squirmed, embarrassed for her.

"A friend gave it to me," Denise said, then bent to rummage around on an end table, coming up with a crushed pack of cigarettes.

"In exchange for the letter?" Tenner asked bluntly.

"The king's letter?" Denise asked, her voice outraged. "Are you nuts?" She looked back to Kat, her expression hurt. "Kat, do you think I had something to do with this?"

Tenner opened his mouth, but Kat silenced him with a stare, then walked over to her friend. "No, I don't," she said gently. "But if you want to help me and help yourself, just tell the detective what he wants to know. Did your new boyfriend give you the money for your condo?"

Her friend tossed down the pack of cigarettes with a curse, then turned tear-filled eyes toward her. "Yes. Is that so bad?"

"No," Kat assured her, laying a hand on her arm. "Just tell the police who it is."

But Denise shook her head miserably. "I can't tell you—I can't tell anyone." A tear slipped down her pale cheek and she roughly brushed it away.

"So it *was* gained illegally," the detective said triumphantly.

"No," Denise snapped. "It was a gift."

"Oh." Tenner made a clicking sound with his cheek. "A Chinatown sugar daddy? You provide, um, attention, and he provides cash?"

Denise snorted. "You've been watching too much television, Tubby."

Tenner's face turned grim. "So who is it, Ms. Womack? You've got ten seconds to give me a name, or I'm placing you under arrest."

The color drained from her face. "You can't do that."

"It wouldn't be your first time in jail, now would it, Ms. Womack?"

Kat heard her inhale sharply, then she stiffened.

Tenner must have sensed her panic. "And we'll find whoever you entertained at Ms. McKray's apartment that night," he said, crossing his arms smugly. "You should have remembered to wipe the prints from the coffee cups."

Denise's shoulders started to shake and she held a fisted hand to her mouth.

"Denise," Kat admonished softly, "just tell us the truth."

After a couple of whimpers, her friend nodded, her nose glowing from unshed tears. "Okay . . . okay." She hiccuped and Kat hurt for having to wring a confidence out of her friend.

Denise inhaled, then exhaled noisily, obviously gathering her strength. "The money was a gift from a lover to help me buy this miserable excuse for an apartment. H-Her name is G-Gloria Handelman."

Kat blinked, then looked at James. He nodded slightly, as if to acknowledge he remembered the woman's name from their earlier conversations.

"A woman?" Tenner croaked in his seemingly infinite capacity for sensitivity. "Who is this Gloria Handelman? The name sounds familiar."

"She worked at the gallery for a few months as an administrator," Kat volunteered, still stunned by Denise's revelation. "Her father is Morris Handelman, and most of the family members are serious collectors of historical documents."

"Not your everyday family hobby," the detective noted.

"Working at Jellico's was Gloria's first paying job, I think, and she only stayed long enough to find and acquire a half-dozen rare manuscripts through the gallery."

"Employee discount?" Tenner asked, popping his gum.

"No, but the job gave her access to the names of

other private collectors, and she knew immediately when documents hit the market."

"Sounds like the primo job for a collector. Why did she quit?"

"I never knew," Kat replied. "But I do know that the Handelmans were to be one of our prime bidders for the king's letter—Gloria's mother wanted it, so Morris was determined to buy it for her."

The detective pulled out a yellowed pocket notebook and pencil stub. "So this Gloria Handelman is familiar with the gallery security?"

Kat glanced sadly at her friend. "Yes."

James stepped toward them. "Denise," he said gently, "was this Handelman woman the same person who had a cup of coffee with you at Kat's Friday night?"

Looking miserable, Denise nodded. "I guess it's pretty obvious why I lied about having company. But I called Gloria to chat and she wanted to come by to give me the check." She smiled sadly at Kat. "I was embarrassed and afraid you would disapprove."

Kat's heart squeezed and she patted her friend's hand.

"Ms. Womack," James continued, "did you see Ms. Handelman take anything from Ms. McKray's bedroom?"

"Absolutely not."

"Did you leave Ms. Handelman alone in the apartment?"

Denise shook her head, then stopped. "No, wait—I ran down to my car to get an art book I'd bought for her."

"Did she have a bag with her?" James pressed. "One large enough to conceal the garments?"

Her brow furrowed, then she bit her lower lip. "A

black athletic bag—she said she'd just come from the gym and didn't want to risk having her racket stolen by leaving it in her car." Her scowl deepened. "But why would she have gone to so much trouble? Her family is richer than the Rockefellers—and the money her dad would have spent on the letter is a drop in the bucket to the Handelmans."

Tenner scribbled furiously. "What time did she leave?"

Denise sniffed, then squinted. "Around eight-thirty. I folded a load of towels after she left, then came back here."

"Were you alone all night?" Tenner asked.

"Yes," Denise said pointedly.

James cleared his throat. "Ms. McKray mentioned that you requested a private tour of the gallery several weeks ago."

Denise reddened and lowered her gaze. "Gloria talks about galleries and museums all the time—I just wanted to be able to converse with her, that's all." Her face crumpled with concern. "Are you going to drag her into all this?"

"Sorry, ma'am," Tenner said, sounding not the least bit sorry. "She'll have to answer some questions, same as you."

Kat felt Denise's hand on her arm. "Kat, I'm sorry I lied, but I honestly didn't think there was any connection to the break-in." She smiled, her eyes watery. "I'd hate to think that Gloria could have done such a thing, but I'd never knowingly withhold evidence that would take the heat off you."

Her heart expanded with affection for her friend. "Don't worry, Denise, everything will be fine." Kat gave her friend a long, rocking hug, during which Denise whispered, "So, are you in love or what?"

Kat pulled back and opened her mouth to protest, but for once, Denise's expression was void of teasing. She decided to be honest, especially since Denise had just bared her soul to an audience of virtual strangers. "I don't know," she murmured sincerely.

A radiant smile bloomed on Denise's face. "Told ya you needed a man," she said in hushed tones.

Tenner scratched himself indiscreetly. "The more we stir this pile, the more it stinks."

James stopped, his hamburger halfway to his mouth. The man had an uncanny sense of bad timing. He glanced sideways at Kat, who bit back a smile as she dipped a french fry in a mountain of catsup.

"The case is certainly more complicated than we first believed," James agreed.

"It's taking longer to get a search warrant for the Handelman woman's apartment." The detective rubbed his grubby thumb over his fingers in a gesture that said "money." "Looks like no one wants to step on their toes." He belched, excused himself, then added. "Another hour—maybe two."

Wincing at his manners, James asked, "Have you checked out everyone at the gallery?"

"Didn't see much use," Tenner said through a mouthful of chili nachos.

Pushing aside his half-eaten burger, James snatched one of Kat's fries and, curious, dipped it in the catsup. "Anyone at the gallery could have taken Kat's key ring, duplicated her apartment key, and returned them without her knowing." He took a tentative bite of the french fry, then pursed his lips in concession to Kat's taste in fast food.

"I've still got that list of employees that Guy Trent came up with," Tenner admitted.

"What about Guy Trent himself?" James asked. "He's practically a black—" Kat dug her elbow sharply into his ribs, stealing his breath. He'd forgotten she'd gone to great lengths to keep her sordid work arrangement private.

The detective wiped his mouth, missing badly. "What's that?"

James straightened and frowned at Kat, but unable to match the intensity of her glare, relented. "Um, black-hearted. He struck me as being an unlikable fellow."

"Why would he sabotage his own place?" Tenner asked.

"The break-in has resulted in a lot of publicity for the gallery," James pointed out. "I'll bet admission sales have increased."

"Temporarily," Kat agreed. "But we expected droves of people for the showing of the letter, plus the gallery would have earned a commission from the auction—a few hundred curiosity seekers can't make up for the money lost."

"What if the letter had turned out to be a fraud?" James asked.

"Then the auction would be canceled, and Lady Mercer would probably receive some token amount from her insurance company."

"And if it's never found?"

"Then the owner would have a case for the full value of the insurance policy, twenty-five thousand if I remember correctly, which the insurer will seek to extract from

Jellico's." She angled her head toward him. "Is Lady Mercer distraught over the loss?"

James grimaced—he had never heard more vile words spew from Tania's mouth than when she had returned his call. In rather *un*-ladylike terms, she had made it very clear she wanted the American woman who had stolen her chance at worldwide celebrity to perish in prison. "She is rightfully concerned about her investment," he remarked. "Detective, did your men fingerprint the compass Kat found at her apartment?"

"Yep—just hers on it, same as the jewelry, same as the security badge."

"Were there any fibers on the clothing? Hair?"

"Just hers."

"Have you sent anyone to Chinatown to see if the letter is floating around?"

Tenner picked his teeth. "No, and that's a pretty good idea, except they clam up tighter than a vir—" He looked at Kat. "The Chinese aren't very talkative around the police."

James glanced at his watch and unfolded himself stiffly from the hard swivel chair. Damn, she'd given him quite a workout this morning. "Page me when you get the warrant and we'll meet you at the Handelman woman's place." He motioned for Kat to bring the remainder of her lunch with her.

"Where're you going, Donovan? I thought we were working on this together." Tenner looked crestfallen, but James wasn't about to expose his local sources to the man. Kat had walked away to dispose of their trash, so James leaned toward the man and said, "We need some time alone."

Looking like a wounded dog, Tenner said, "High

time to be thinking with your crotch, Donovan. We got a case to solve."

Smirking, James said, "I'm trained to keep several plates in the air at once, Tenner."

Tenner frowned as Kat walked up to the table.

"Ready?" James's gaze raked her glorious figure with appreciation. She was demurely tucked into tailored slacks and a high-collared shirt, topped with a sensible wool jacket. Her hair was fastened back in a tight wad, and her wire-rimmed glasses perched on the end of her nose. Only a discriminating eye would recognize what lay beneath the plain brown wrapping. Snatches of their morning tumble surfaced in his mind and he suddenly wished they were indeed off to share a romantic tryst.

Thankfully oblivious to his lusty thoughts, she grabbed her purse. "Where are we going?" she asked when they reached the sidewalk.

He forced his mind back to the case. The sooner he wrapped up this mess, the sooner he could leave San Francisco. And the sooner he left San Francisco, the sooner he could shake these visions of cold English nights with Kat curled up next to him.

Ah, New York . . . a city where he could immerse himself in fun, frivolity, and anonymity for a few weeks. New York would be the perfect place to distract him from these discomfiting thoughts of becoming . . . what was the word he was looking for? *Monogamous.* James shuddered.

"James?" Kat's voice yanked him from his train of thought. "Where are we going?"

He stared into her blue eyes for several seconds, perturbed by the power she wielded over his psyche. "To resolve this predicament as quickly as possible," he said brusquely. "I have no intention of staying here forever."

TEN

Kat was so troubled by James's comment that she nearly plowed into him when he stopped abruptly at a pay phone. He pulled a handful of change from his pocket and picked through it. "I've always found American coins to be confusing—let's see, a twenty pence and a nickel to make a telephone call?"

She grinned. "If we had a twenty pence." He relaxed his sudden ill mood long enough for a wry smile. She fished through the silver in his hand. "Here, try a quarter. Who are you calling?"

"An associate," he said, his tone all business. He turned his body to exclude her from the conversation, but she stepped close and listened anyway, her feelings smarting. Her little theory about the "morning-after syndrome" was kicking in—and apparently the malady was universal.

"This is Agent James Donovan, on assignment in San Francisco. I need to speak with Antonio, please. The code word is 'Black Mulligan.' . . . Yes, I'll wait."

Kat's pulse picked up. Code word? Did they really say stuff like that?

"Antonio? Agent James Donovan here. Good to speak with you again too. I'm in town looking into the disappearance of a piece of fine art, and have reason to believe it may have been sold on the black market. . . . Yes. . . . Very good. I'll be there, with a—" he paused and Kat's ears perked up. "With a female companion. Thank you."

He hung up and Kat stepped away, feigning fascination with a banged-up coffee table in the window of an antique shop.

"A future project?"

She turned and gave him a crooked smile. "Maybe my own business one of these days. A girl's got to pay the rent somehow."

"So you won't be going back to Jellico's?"

She shook her head slowly, suddenly melancholy for all the years that Jellico's had been her second home. "Even if Guy would take me back, it's time for me to move on."

His brow creased. "Will you stay in the city?"

"I'm not sure. I have a friend in Los Angeles who's been trying to get me to come work for him for years." She gestured to the phone. "Are you finished?"

"Yes," he said, rolling his wrist to check his watch. "And we have an appointment in Chinatown in thirty minutes."

He handed her a card with the name and address printed neatly and she nodded. "With whom?"

"Someone who will keep an eye out for the infamous letter."

"Who?"

James sighed. "I don't know his name, and for the love of God, don't ask him when we get there."

Going to Chinatown to meet a stranger who moved in the underworld of the black market. It was all so, so . . . clandestine. Her heart pounded with excitement, her skin tingled with anticipation. Slinging her purse over her shoulder, she said, "Let's go."

"I'll hail a cab," he said, stepping to the curb.

"James, you're in San Francisco. Van Ness is just a couple of blocks over—we'll take the trolley and still get there in plenty of time." His car was still at the police station.

He grimaced. "I'm afraid that's not my style."

"Fine," she said, pushing up her glasses. "I'll meet you there." Then she turned and started walking. There was nothing worse than a moody man.

"Kat!" he called, his voice flat with impatience. His second attempt sounded more cordial. "Kat, I need the address—I don't even know where this place is."

She turned, walking backward and farther away from him with her hands raised, palms up. "Guess you're going to have to depend on me for a while, Agent Donovan."

His mouth twisted in resignation, and he began walking after her. "Okay . . . uncle." He caught up to her in a few strides but his face remained stoic. Kat felt burdensome for preempting his trip to New York, and disappointed that his demeanor toward her had changed so drastically since this morning.

Then she kicked herself mentally. What had she expected? That this morning would mean something to him? When would she learn that men were simple creatures driven by base needs . . . regardless if they were American, European, or Martian. Take James for instance—strip away his impeccable clothes and his suave accent, and what was left?

Kat winced. A gorgeous, naked, mute man with a big gun.

So why did sex have to change things? Because it erased the thrill of the chase? Didn't the thrill of the catch count anymore?

Biting back a sigh, she chalked up another one to experience. Right now, though, she needed this man's help. So she swallowed her wounded feelings, donned a cheerful smile, and played tour guide, indicating shops and other points of interest along the way. After a few minutes, James seemed to relax, asking questions about the local architecture. By the time they'd reached the trolley stop, he seemed to be in better spirits.

"Sit or stand?" she asked, climbing onto a red car the size of a small school bus. Clear vinyl window covers had been rolled down in deference to the mild weather, funneling a salty breeze across the passengers' faces.

"Stand," he said, wrapping one large hand around a pole. The driver rang a bell, then the car lurched into motion, heading directly downhill.

"You have to lean out to get the best view," she yelled, showing him. The sensation of hurtling into the heart of the city with the wind blowing on her face was a thrill she never tired of, even though she'd experienced it dozens, perhaps hundreds of times since childhood. The car moved at a speed just slow enough to allow a passing glimpse of the stunning homes and businesses on either side of the street, but fast enough to cause her stomach to flutter.

To her surprise, James seemed to be enjoying it too. A smile creased his face as he leaned out precariously far, the wind tousling his thick dark hair and flapping his tailored sport coat. His head pivoted to take in their surroundings.

Watching him, Kat's breath caught in her throat. He was an enigma to her, this man. Scary yet safe, powerful yet vulnerable, sexy yet professional . . . her mind was crowded with the impact of his synergy, the whole person. She was sadly aware that his affection, attraction—whatever he'd felt for her—was dwindling rapidly as he became increasingly anxious to be on his way.

The architecture and store frontage abruptly changed under Asian influence as they rolled into the outskirts of Chinatown. Often mistaken for a simple tourist haven, even Kat had to remind herself that above the souvenir shops and restaurants, entire families lived in the confines of one or two small rooms.

"The next stop is ours," she said loudly, and he indicated he'd heard her.

When the car squealed to a stop, they jumped down, Kat's cheeks stinging from the exhilarating ride.

"A most commendable mode of transportation, Ms. McKray," James conceded with a smile, running his fingers through his hair.

Gratified, Kat pointed down a sidewalk crowded with shoppers and street vendors. "The bakery is down this street and around the corner." As they walked toward their meeting place, Kat's pulse picked up. "Do you think whoever stole the letter sold it already?"

James shrugged. "If the Handelman woman took it, she would have kept it. But if someone else—let's say your boss—stole it or arranged to have it stolen, then chances are good they would have gotten rid of it as soon as possible."

"So you don't think Gloria Handelman did it?"

"I'm simply covering all bases so the thief doesn't benefit from time spent on chasing misleading clues."

"And you still suspect my boss?"

James pursed his lips and lifted one black brow. "After that miserable performance at the polygraph machine this morning, perhaps I should still suspect you."

Kat nearly stumbled, unable to meet his gaze. "I was just nervous, that's all—I told you I didn't steal that damned letter."

"That's fortunate, because Lady Mercer is out for blood."

"I can't blame her," Kat said with sincerity, wondering if speaking with his supposedly former lover had something to do with his distance. Maybe the woman was still a fixture in his life, or at least in his heart.

"This is the place," she announced, stopping at a white building with a winged window front, full of colorful baked goodies. Double doors were propped open to handle the flow of foot traffic.

"Smells good," he said. "We're a little early—how about coffee?"

She nodded, craning her neck to scrutinize the people sitting at the half-full tables near the back, expecting to see a man dressed in a trench coat, with a fedora pulled low over his eyes.

"Why don't you get us a table? And try to be less conspicuous, Miss Marple." He turned toward the tall glass counter.

Kat frowned at his back, then chose a table for four in the corner, farthest from the door and near the bathrooms. At the counter, James bent at the waist, pointed to something behind the glass case, and held up two fingers to the elderly woman who waited on him.

She glanced around the nondescript walls dotted

with cheap Oriental art and perused the lackluster tables and chairs. She wondered how many secretly arranged meetings had taken place here, perhaps even at this very table. She wiped her moist hands on a paper napkin from the holder on the table and tried to relax.

James approached her, holding two paper cups of coffee in his joined hands and a small wax bag under his elbow. "I thought we might have a treat," he said.

Kat leaned forward and lowered her voice. "Is he here?"

James looked at her pointedly. "No, he isn't." He took a seat across from hers. "You might have picked a cleaner spot."

Frowning at the tabletop, her defenses rose. "Well, it looks clean to me."

"Ma'am," James called to the woman behind the counter who had waited on him. "Would you be so kind as to send someone out to wipe our table?"

He was a neat freak, she decided, straining to see whatever it was on the shiny Formica table that concerned him.

A young girl emerged from behind the glass food display, brandishing a wet cloth and offering them a shy smile. "So sorry," she said, her English only slightly influenced by a Chinese accent.

"No problem," Kat felt obliged to offer as she lifted her cup for the girl to scrub vigorously beneath.

"Do you have a photo of the item, sir?" the girl asked so smoothly and quietly, Kat almost didn't hear her. When she realized they had met their informant, she snapped up her head to stare. Only after she felt James pressing the toe of his shoe down on hers did she force herself to relax and look away from the girl—who couldn't have been more than sixteen.

"Unfortunately, no picture," James replied, taking a sip of the coffee and not looking directly at her. "It's a three-page letter on yellow parchment, the dimensions of each sheet about five by seven inches. Written in German, the letter is unsigned, but reputed to have been authored by King George III to a paramour."

"When did it disappear?"

"Friday night, just after midnight, from a gallery called Jellico's. Estimated worth on the market, twenty thousand dollars."

"And where can you be reached?"

"Flagiron Hotel, under the name Donovan—James Donovan."

At the sound of him announcing his name, a shiver raised the hair on Kat's arms.

"There," the girl said in a louder voice, giving the table a final swipe. "So sorry for the inconvenience, sir."

"Thank you," he said, inclining his dark head in a curt nod. He remained silent as she walked away and calmly opened the wax paper bag to withdraw a dry, speckled cookie. "Would you like a biscuit for your coffee?" he asked Kat, as if nothing had transpired.

"Um, yes," she said, reaching into the bag and taking the other one. She studied his impassive face as he broke the cookie in two and took a crumbly bite.

"This is your life, isn't it?" she asked, hearing the wonder in her own voice.

A tiny frown crimped the area between his eyebrows. "What do you mean?"

"Secret phone calls, informants, guns, investigations—you know, high drama."

"You make it sound glamorous," he said with a small laugh.

"Isn't it?"

He chewed another bite of cookie before answering. "It isn't boring, but it's far from glamorous, I assure you."

"But the travel, the danger—"

"Is exhausting," he said, punctuated by an abbreviated nod. "I'm rather glad to be rid of it full-time."

"So from now on, you can pick and choose your assignments?"

He nodded, his smile satisfied. "In fact, I took this job primarily to learn a bit about the fine arts industry. I have a job offer at the Webster museum in London to look into some improprieties, but I had little better than a layman's understanding." He took a sip of the coffee, then another. "Mr. Muldoon was kind enough to give me a crash course during our lengthy flight, and you have added to my knowledge as well." He gave her hand a friendly pat, as if she were a helpful pet instead of the woman with whom he'd most recently shared his body.

"So you're going to take the London museum job?" she asked, her heart contracting at the thought of him returning to England.

"If I ever get to leave this place," he said, revealing one dimple in a dry half-grin. He bent his head and pressed a button on his silent pager, then frowned.

"Is that Tenner?" she asked, finishing her coffee. She felt a crushing urgency to solve the case and release James from his inconvenient obligation.

"No, I was just checking to see if I'd missed a call," he said. "And I wonder what's taking so bloody long."

"According to Denise, Gloria doesn't live far from here, so we can get there in no time. Let's take a walk."

He shrugged, exhibiting typical male disinterest in window-shopping. "Sure."

But Kat wasn't interested in shopping either—she

simply wanted to escape the intimate setting of the bakery where they were forced to converse over a tiny table. She didn't like this push-pull feel radiating between them; it was too awkward and too draining.

She set off in the direction of the trolley car, walking slowly to hide the turmoil inside her head. They strolled by several T-shirt shops, a butcher shop that featured some pretty unappetizing fare hanging in the window, and a few furniture stores. Outside one of the more up-scale boutiques, Kat stopped by a rack of men's fine silk ties and fingered through them, thinking of Valmer. He'd already told her he wouldn't accept money for her representation, but she wanted to give him some small token of her thankfulness.

"I'm going to buy this for Val," she said, selecting a teal-colored tie with tiny yellow shadow boxes.

"Nice," James agreed, walking his fingers through several on the rack. She really was very thoughtful, he decided, thinking he probably should select a gift for his sister while he had the time. He followed Kat inside, pausing to allow his eyes to adjust to the dim interior. She definitely had chosen one of the nicer shops—marble floors, twinkling chandeliers. An impressive array of clothing, jewelry, intricate china, and art spilled upward to a second story.

A tall glass cabinet filled with figurines caught his eye and he made his way toward it. Most of the statues were various forms of Oriental erotica: nude figures, both sexes, separate but entwineable in various positions to form an add-on orgy of massive proportions if the collector desired. Like the diversity of the human body, some of the primitive figurines boasted flamboyant breasts and genitals, some were nearly androgynous. Jade pervaded, but wood, black soapstone, and even ivory were shown, with staggering price tags.

"I see you found the good stuff," Kat said near his shoulder. She held a small paper bag under her arm as she returned her wallet to her purse.

"Most intriguing," he admitted, a bit flustered from her sudden appearance. "Are these common?"

"Not this quality."

"Quite dear," he noted, indicating the price tags.

"And these are fairly new pieces," she added. "Antique erotica figurines bring astronomical prices. Jellico's buys every one we can get our hands on, but the old ones rarely come on the market."

"I rather like these," James said. "Would you help me choose a couple of pieces?"

Her head swung around, her eyes slightly questioning. Looking into those blue depths, James saw something that struck terror in his heart: a nucleus around which to build a future. For the first time in his life, he felt . . . did he dare even think it? Defenseless.

"I'm asking for your professional advice on an investment," he assured her, detaching himself from the implied intimacy surrounding the figurines.

She pressed her lips together, nodding. "Of course. What is your price range?"

"My price range is the cost of whichever two you choose."

"I didn't realize you were a collector."

"I'm not," he confessed. "Simply because I've never before found anything I deemed worth collecting."

Giving him a small smile, she turned and waved for a sales clerk. Once the cabinet was open, she accepted a pair of cotton gloves from the woman and walked around the cabinet, scrutinizing every piece on the four shelves.

He watched her move—her brow furrowed in concentration, her eyes alight with excitement—and again he was struck by the sensuality she exuded. She picked up a few of the figures one by one, weighed them in her gloved hand, then examined them closely. A couple she even went so far as to caress, paying special attention to a standing jade male about ten inches tall, thick through the shoulders and thighs and heavily sexed. His arms, crudely fashioned but effectively rendered, were slightly lifted, as if he were reaching out to someone.

She replaced the figure, and looked up. "Do you have a preference?"

He smiled and crossed his arms, enjoying himself immensely. "Actually, I was thinking one male and one female."

Kat gave him a wry smile, then nudged aside a kneeling ivory male to select a wooden female, lying on her side, knees bent. "I had assumed that much, but as far as the materials are concerned, or the . . . um . . . the positions?"

She blushed adorably, he decided. "All of the materials are superb. And as far as the positions go"—he grinned and splayed his hands—"I don't discriminate."

"D-Do you have a special place in mind to display them?" she asked, turning her attention back to the cabinet.

"My library, or perhaps my bedroom," he said, but instead of picturing the statues on display, all he could conjure up were images of Kat moving through his big, drafty home, adding warmth in her wake. He forced his attention back to the present, and noticed she had once again returned to the big jade male.

"I like him too," he announced, causing her to glance up.

She frowned. "He doesn't seem to have a partner, though. As magnificent as they are, all the females seem so . . . so insignificant next to him."

The Chinese saleswoman, who had faded into the background, made a clucking noise. "Very observant— the owner has the female in his office upstairs."

James pursed his lips. "May we see her?"

The woman hesitated, then nodded curtly. "I will bring her."

The instant he saw her, James wanted her. Buxom and lush-hipped, her hair pooled behind her on the ground to counterbalance her arched body, thrust forward to meet her missing partner. When the clerk set her in front of the male, her energy flowed into his. They might have been carved from the same stone, a perfect complement . . . yin and yang.

"How much?" James asked, striving to keep the urgency out of his voice.

The woman remained silent for several seconds, her gaze straight ahead, her mouth twisting in thought. James caught Kat's gaze and, wondering if he should make an offer, lifted his eyebrows. But she answered with an almost imperceptible shake of her head.

Another moment passed, and the woman seemed to be struggling with her decision. At last, she nodded and named a price—double the price of the male, but half of what James had been willing to pay.

"Done," he said, relief and something akin to joy filling his chest. After the woman secured the cabinet, James also selected one of the silk shawls for his sister, glad when Kat seconded his choice of black and silver.

"That was quite a coup," Kat said when the woman disappeared to pack the treasures.

"I'm rather pleased," he admitted. "Thank you for your inspiration."

Confusion flitted over her face and she shook her head. "You cinched the deal."

"Ah, but you have given me a heightened awareness for beautiful things." Wispy baby hair, dislodged from her bun by the trolley ride, framed her face. Her eyes were luminous, making him want to get to the person hiding behind those spectacles. That woman in his arms this morning.

She laughed. "If I have stirred your interest in launching a collection, then I'm pleased."

James opened his mouth to tell her exactly which of his interests she had stirred, but the woman returned, carrying two plain brown boxes, a wide smile on her face. "It's the last time they will be separated. After this, I know you will keep them together."

Nodding in assurance, James handed her a gold credit card and said, "I hope the owner isn't too distressed when he finds her missing."

The woman wrinkled her nose and dismissed his concern with a wave of her hand. "He's my husband, and he doesn't deserve her."

He felt touched that the woman was willing to anger her spouse in order to see the "couple" together—and awed that the woman trusted him to honor the pair's bond.

The woman walked around the counter and handed one box to James, one to Kat, then tucked the bag with the shawl beneath his arm. "Happiness to you both," she said as they left the store, and it struck him that she thought he and Kat were a couple too.

He had never been part of a couple, and the label wrapped around him like a starched flannel robe straight from the clothier's—rather ill-fitting and uncomfortable, but tolerable because it had the potential of becoming a favored garment.

Out on the sidewalk, Kat smirked in his direction. "That was a very expensive little trip."

"But worth it," James proclaimed, happier than in recent memory. He felt a faint vibration at his waist. "And that must be Tenner," he said, nodding to his pager. For once the detective's timing was perfect.

ELEVEN

Gloria Handelman was also a late riser, Kat noted wryly, considering the afternoon hour of three o'clock was nearly half spent when the woman answered the door in roomy striped pajamas. Kat would have recognized her, but the changes she'd made to herself were blatantly irreverent—perhaps part of a "coming out" statement?

She was a thin, angular person, boyishly built and sporting cropped, peroxide-white hair. At least ten earrings studded the rims of both ears. When Tenner waved his badge, she yawned widely and held her temple as if she had a headache. Or a hangover.

"You better not be selling Amway," she said, her thin, crooked eyebrows crumpled together.

"Ms. Handelman, we have a search warrant for your apartment. I'm Detective Tenner from the city police department. This is Agent James Donovan and—"

"Katherine?" The woman's eyes widened, her smudged brows climbing. "What the hell is going on?"

Kat stepped forward. "There was a break-in at Jellico's Friday night."

The woman's mouth twisted and she nodded. "Oh, yeah—the letter. Dad called and said Mom was inconsolable, then asked what the hell he was going to do about a birthday gift. I suggested getting her a woman, but he wasn't amused."

Kat smiled awkwardly, trying to squash the image of this woman with her best friend. "Detective Tenner would like to ask you some questions—may we come in?"

Officers Campbell and Raines didn't wait for an answer, but simply stepped into the apartment and split up. Gloria gave them a murderous look. "Know that anything you morons break is probably worth both your salaries for a year." She turned back to the door and squinted. "Detective, um, Tenner, is it? Do you know who my father is?"

"Yep . . . listen, can I use your bathroom?" He leaned forward, patting his protruding stomach, and loudly whispered, "I think I should've skipped the onions on the chili burger."

Kat swallowed a smile and James coughed. Gloria's lip curled in disgust. "There's a gas station across the street."

He grunted. "Guess I'll wait. But we still need to talk."

Anger lit her eyes, then she stepped back, sweeping her arm magnanimously. "I don't know how I can help, but sure, come on in—what is this, Sunday afternoon?"

Gloria's apartment was breathtaking, filled with expensive, smart furnishings and dressed in an offbeat flair that Kat bet was Gloria's doing, and no designer's. And she was either very neat or employed a maid.

"I'm sure you'll understand if I don't offer you a seat," she said, smiling tightly.

"That's all right," Tenner said, then winced and rubbed his stomach again. "I'd better stand. Now then, can you account for your whereabouts Saturday morning between the hours of midnight and one o'clock in the morning?"

Confusion clouded her pale eyes and she shook her head slightly. "Wait a minute—you think *I* broke into the museum?" She laughed in high-pitched, hysterical amusement and lowered herself into an armless leopard-skin chair. "Detective, that is the most fun I've been accused of in a while."

"So you have an alibi?" Tenner pressed.

She smiled dreamily, as if a life of crime was a direction she hadn't considered, but might give serious thought. Then she looked heavenward. "Let's see, I was at Barishka's Friday night—or was that last night?" She glanced back to Tenner. "No, I'm sure it was Friday. Dragged myself home around three or three-thirty."

"That's a lesbian bar right?"

Gloria nodded. "Lesbians, drag queens, and wide-eyed, sight-seeing heteros."

"Did you go to the bar after you visited Denise Womack at Ms. McKray's apartment?" the detective asked, pursing his lips.

She gave Kat a surprised look. "Oh, you know about that. Well, I for one am glad it's out in the open, although I'm not sure Denise is ready to deal with it just yet. She's worried about what you'll think, Katherine."

"What prompted your visit to Ms. McKray's?" James asked, breaking his silence for the first time.

Gloria flicked her eyes over him appreciatively. "To give Denise a check for a down payment on her condo—why she wants the dump, though, I can't fathom."

Tenner grunted. "Did she need the check that night?"

She shook her head. "I think she has a few weeks to get the money together. But Kat's place is on the way to the club where I work out, and I wanted to give Denise some peace of mind. We had a cup of coffee and cold pizza."

"Detective," Officer Raines interrupted, holding up a large black gym bag he'd pulled from a coat closet. Tenner walked over to retrieve it, then unzipped it and rifled through the contents.

"If you're looking for dirty underwear, you're out of luck," Gloria offered dryly.

"Ms. Handelman," James said, crossing his arms, "would you mind telling us why you left Jellico's?"

Gloria shrugged her bony shoulders. "Boredom—oh, sometimes it was exciting, but the day-in, day-out stuff was a drag."

"Yeah," Tenner chimed in. "Working for a living stinks, doesn't it?"

Her thin mouth pulled back into an arrogant smile.

He handed the bag back to Raines, then frowned at Gloria. "Ms. McKray tells us your family wanted that letter badly . . . bad enough for you to steal it?"

Kat shifted nervously at the expression on Gloria's face. Tenner was treading on thin ice—the woman could have him for a snack if she wanted.

"Detective, my parents derive their enjoyment of having an expensive manuscript collection from being able to display it prominently and make all their rich friends green with envy. I can assure you they have no interest in something which has to be squirreled away for fear of prosecution."

"What about you?"

"I'm only interested in Victorian correspondence between homosexual lovers—if it turns out he wrote the letter to a man, call me. And as far as hiding anything—" Her gaze cut to James. "Everything about me is available for inspection."

One of James's dimples appeared and Kat felt an irrational zing of jealousy.

Tenner was growing impatient. "I'll need the names of people who saw you at Barishka's around midnight."

She shrugged again, searching her memory. "Everyone on the staff knows me, and the regular weekend customers were there—wait a minute." A wicked smile crept across her face. "Here's the name of someone you might know . . . Ronald Beaman."

Shock bolted through Kat. "Ronald?"

"Jellico's head of security?" James asked.

Gloria nodded, pleased with herself. "Ron likes to dress up on his nights off—he has a bent toward long, feminine skirts and high heels."

Tenner expelled a noisy sigh and scratched his head. "Wigs?"

"Dark, shoulder-length. Looks pretty good too."

The detective winced. "Damn."

"Sunday is a big night at Barishka's—they have a drag queen pageant at seven, with talent competition and everything." She winked. "And Ron does a great Tina Turner impression."

James felt more than a little self-conscious standing offstage with Tenner and Kat, waiting for Ron Beaman to finish a teeth-jarring rendition of a song Kat identified as "Proud Mary." The detective had wanted to catch him off guard, and from the gaped expression on the man's face when he skipped off stage, blowing kisses to the audience, Tenner had certainly achieved his goal.

"Nice duds, Beaman," Tenner said sarcastically.

"H-How . . ." The security guard was speechless, his hand to his fake bosom, his eyes darting from face to face.

"Never mind how," Tenner barked. "Where were you Friday night between midnight and one o'clock?"

"H-Here," Ronald whispered, dragging the wig from his head to reveal a stocking cap. Without the hair, his fake eyelashes and heavy makeup looked clownish.

"I'll take that," the detective snapped, grasping the wig by thumb and forefinger, his mouth twisted in disgust. "And you're lying because the bartender already told us you left before midnight."

Moisture welled up in Beaman's eyes.

"Okay . . . okay. I left w-with a man. I'll give you his name, but you have to promise not to go to his house." A tear slid down his rouged cheek. "His wife doesn't know and neither does mine."

"Don't even think about skipping town," Tenner warned, shaking the wig at him. "If we've been on a damned wild-goose chase and it turns out you're the bird, your wife's reaction to your sideline will be the least of your worries, Tina."

Gloria Handelman, dressed in a painful-looking sling of black leather, lifted her hand in a little wave from the bar as they made their way toward the door, then added punctuation by giving Tenner the finger.

"I think she digs me," he said as they walked outside.

The man was as smart as a tree, James decided. "Maybe you should join her," he suggested. "That is, unless we can come up with just one more lead suspect before midnight," he added sarcastically.

The detective snorted. "Think it was Beaman?"

James shook his head slowly. "I'd be surprised, although he could have been in on it with someone else."

"Ms. McKray," Tenner said, turning toward her. "Do you have any theories?"

Kat jerked her head up. "Are you saying, Detective, that you no longer think I'm involved?"

He nodded. "That's right. We might never catch the person who staged that break-in, but I'm not about to see an innocent woman go to jail. I'll make a call to Ms. Pena's office in the morning to ask her to drop the charges."

Relief flooded James's body at the same time Kat's face erupted into smiles, her openmouthed laughter music to his ears. Yet even as he gave her shoulders a squeeze, James felt his chest constrict. Should he leave now? The letter wasn't much closer to being found, yet somehow he felt as if his duty had been done. But, then why did he feel torn?

"Come on, I'll give you both a lift," Tenner said, taking Kat's elbow. "His hotel and your apartment are on my way."

"Well, actually," Kat said, biting her lower lip, "I'm staying at the Flagiron."

Tenner lifted an eyebrow, but didn't say anything.

"In my own room," she added hurriedly. "And just until I get the locks changed on my doors tomorrow."

"Good idea," Tenner said as they stopped by his faded car. "Considering someone was able to waltz in and out of there like they knew the place."

James held open the front passenger door for Kat, then claimed the seat behind her in the boat-size, four-door sedan. The inside smelled moldy and he was rather glad the interior light had expired so he couldn't see what scuffed and rattled beneath his feet.

The detective rolled into the front seat. "So, Agent Donovan, when is a good time tomorrow for me and you to question this guy who's supposedly fooling around with Beaman?"

James realized with a start that at some point, the detective had passed him the lead in handling the investigation. Just when he was thinking of making his escape to New York . . . his escape *from* Katherine McKray. "I'm not sure of my schedule at the moment," he said vaguely. "I'll call you, Detective."

The ride to the hotel seemed interminable to James. Kat was talkative, no doubt buoyed by news of her impending freedom, and Tenner apologized for his men making such a mess of her apartment. When she responded that she would be moving soon anyway, James pursed his lips in thought. So she had decided to take the job in Los Angeles. Well, jolly good for her.

He sat back against the seat and crossed his arms, frowning as something crunched beneath his left hip. Now when he remembered their brief time together in San Francisco, he couldn't picture her moving around in her apartment, or listening to the jazz band at Torbett's, or leaning over the side of a trolley car, smiling into the wind.

Instead she'd be in Los Angeles breathing smog and getting shot at on the crowded roadways. He scoffed silently. Foolish woman—didn't she know how dangerous it would be to live there all alone?

"L.A. is terrific," Tenner said. "Lots of nightlife, and celebrities everywhere. Young, pretty girl like you will love it—might even marry yourself a movie star."

While Kat murmured her thanks, James resisted the

temptation to lean forward and bop the man on the top of his round head.

"Here we are," the detective said cheerfully, throwing the car into park with a lurch.

"You don't have to get out," James assured him, scrambling out to open Kat's door.

But Tenner emerged and walked around to the trunk, holding up a key. "Don't forget about your boxes—I wouldn't want my wife to think I'd bought her a gift or something." He laughed and slapped James on the back.

James couldn't hide his surprise. "You're married?"

"Hell, yes. Eighteen years. Three great kids—all girls." He pulled up his polyester pants and rocked back on his heels.

Good God, out of all the women in this gigantic country, how had Tenner managed to bumble onto the one girl who was desperate enough to marry him? And worse—James gulped—*sleep* with him, at least three times.

"Most wonderful woman on the face of the earth," Tenner said, his voice growing uncharacteristically warm. "Can't wait to get home—she always has a nice hot cup of Ovaltine waiting for me. 'Night, folks."

Kat shifted the box she held to her hip and watched Tenner drive away. "How sweet."

James grunted, realized he sounded like Tenner, then said, "Some people thrive on domesticity." He hadn't meant to sound quite so disdainful, but there it was and he couldn't take it back.

Kat tipped her head back and looked into his eyes. "And some people thrive on arrogance." Then she turned and marched toward the hotel entrance.

James followed, feeling lumpy and grumpy, and caught up with her at the elevator. "I apologize," he said, suddenly feeling tired. "Perhaps the time change is affecting me after all."

She was quiet for a full moment, the tension crackling across the few feet between them. "Perhaps you just can't understand how a man could be happy going home to the same woman every day." The elevator door dinged open and she stepped in first.

When she turned around, he grinned broadly. "That's true."

But she obviously didn't share his humor. Blocking his entrance, she said, "No, James, that's sad."

Then she pressed a button and the door slid shut.

James scowled at the closed steel door, then stabbed at the up button to retrieve another empty car. When he unlocked his door, he found the box she'd carried upstairs sitting inside the connecting door—the panel on his side was standing open, hers was closed. And locked, he'd bet. The saleswoman had printed "Woman" and "Man" on the respective boxes. He exhaled noisily and carried his own Man box over to the desk, then stored his sister's gift.

As he removed his jacket and retrieved the television remote, his ears strained for sounds coming from her room. Nothing. James stacked the four bed pillows against the headboard, then slipped off his shoes and stretched out on the bed.

His muscles sighed in relief and various joints popped and cracked as he sought a comfortable position. He was getting old, he thought wryly. Old and crotchety.

He clicked through the channels, stopping briefly at an adult movie before frowning and going on to the news. It would do him good to be reminded that more important things were going on in the world, that he had isolated himself, making this little burglary case—and Kat—seem more significant than they really were. After all, in the scheme of things, it was one nonviolent crime, and she was one woman.

To prove his point, he reached for the phone and set it on his stomach, then dialed the airline and booked a first-class seat on a direct flight to New York Monday night at eleven-thirty. He hung up with a smile of satisfaction on his face, but it was short-lived.

His traitorous eyes strayed to the Woman box on the floor. Females were such complex creatures—changing moods at the drop of a hat, first giving, then withholding, seductive one minute, uptight the next—how did any man stick it out? The ones who did, didn't know any better, he decided, nodding to the Man box on the desk for support.

They didn't know there was a world out there to travel, full of beautiful women and good food and wonderful adventures. Didn't know that admitting vulnerability to a woman meant transferring the power to her—the power to woo or wound, as she saw fit.

He glanced back to the Woman box, remembering her curvaceous lines with a rush of pleasure, then bit down on the inside of his cheek. Kat's naked image rose up to mock him, the involuntary hardening of his sex a taunting reinforcement of his earlier observation of power between the sexes. The Maker had tempered a woman's package by coupling a vexing will with a tantalizing body. Which was the bottom line, really. Their trump card. They had what men needed, and all the cat-and-mouse games in between revolved around it.

James dropped his head back on the pillows and admitted defeat to the ceiling fan. Then he pulled himself up, retrieved Woman and sat her on the desk next to

Man. "They've got us, but good," he mumbled to his jade counterpart.

He stepped back into his shoes, then walked to the door connecting their rooms and, after a few seconds' hesitation, knocked.

It was nearly a minute before he detected movement on the other side. "Who is it?" she asked.

Case in point, James noted wryly. "An arrogant man bearing apologies."

Silence, then "Apology accepted."

He closed his eyes in frustration, then said, "I'm leaving tomorrow night, Pussy-Kat."

Several seconds of tense silence passed, then the lock on her door made a thwacking sound and she pulled open the door.

James blinked. She wore a long, white sleeveless gown of thin knit, reminiscent of a floor-length fitted T-shirt. Except the innocence of the fabric and the demure neckline was corrupted by the deep armholes and thigh-high slit on either side. Her hair was captured in a low side ponytail, loosely gathered beneath her ear.

"I was ready for bed," she said, her smile a bit shaky.

All moisture had left his mouth. "So I see," he managed to croak.

"So you're leaving tomorrow," she said, suddenly fascinated with the doorknob she held.

He cleared his throat. "Yes, I, um . . . I'm no longer needed here."

She glanced up, and he tried desperately to read her eyes. "You're not going to try to find the letter?"

"Our friend in Chinatown will stand a much better chance than I."

"And if it isn't located?"

He shrugged. "Then Lady Mercer will collect a few

thousand pounds from the insurance company and perhaps an asterisk next to her name in a book someday."

Kat inhaled deeply, straining the nearly transparent
fabric. Her nipples were clearly outlined, pebbled from
the room's chill, he supposed. His body, indifferent to
the cold that had triggered her reaction, began to harden
in response to something else.

She laughed softly. "This has been the most eventful
three days of my life."

His, too, but in a different way. James reached for her
hand and twined her warm fingers with his, then leaned
close, his body surging with desire, and whispered,
"Let's top it off with an eventful night, shall we?"

After a heartbeat's hesitation, she nodded and opened
her mouth to accept his kiss. Within moments they were
on her bed, tearing at each other's clothes. James told
himself to wait, to love her with steeping slowness, a
memory to savor in the months to come. But when she
lay bare against him, beneath him, astride him, his re-
straint fled. Her mouth, hands, and silken passage tore
the energy from his body with staggering speed and intensity. He gathered her against him and gasped,
"Kat . . . Kat . . . my Kat."

She quieted and was soon breathing evenly beside
him, her head tucked beneath his arm. Exhausted, but
wide awake, he stared at her incredible breasts rising and
falling until he felt the beginning of another erection and
decided to get a drink of water.

After easing from the bed, he padded across the
room, retrieving his clothing on the way back to his
room. He tossed the garments on the bed, ran a glass of
water in the bathroom, and drained it. When he
emerged, he decided it would be a good time to call Lady

Mercer and tell her of his plans to leave the city. He felt sure she would agree there was little more he could do.

Squashing the nagging thought that he was running away from Kat more than the investigation, he dialed the numbers and waited for the connection.

"Lady Tania Mercer's residence."

James recognized the voice of the housekeeper. "Mary, this is James Donovan. I need to speak with Tania—is she available?"

"She left for the London cottage, sir, and she has yet to install a phone there. But I expect her back any day—shall I take a message?"

James frowned. "Yes, Mary, thank you. Please tell her that I've left the matter of the missing letter in the hands of the police and I'll be traveling to New York Monday evening. I'll call her when I get settled in on Tuesday."

"Fine, Mr. Donovan, I'll tell her."

James returned the handset and briefly wondered if he were letting Tania down by not trying to locate that damned silly love letter. Glancing toward Kat's room, James wondered at what point his mission had shifted from solving the crime to seeing her cleared.

When she'd asked him to get her father's humidor, he decided. He would never forget the panic in her eyes when she thought she might lose something so precious to her. James walked over to his closet, then knelt and dialed in the combination of the wall safe. The door popped open, revealing a cavity not much larger than the humidor itself. The rich scent of the mahogany tickled his nostrils as he carefully withdrew the box.

Since he'd be leaving tomorrow, he would check the water one last time and place the humidor in Kat's room. He lifted the lid and noted on the barometer that the moisture level had dropped just below the proper level of seventy percent. He removed the soapsize sponge from a vented cavity and wet it under the faucet. That done, he couldn't resist fingering the wonderful cigars again.

He chose one and twirled it between thumb and forefinger, loving the feel of it, the flash of the gold band, the colorful label. Which seemed to be loose, he noticed, then stopped when something fluttered to the carpet.

James bent over to pick up the tiny square of paper, realizing when he turned it over that it was a stamp. A very old stamp. And he recalled Guy Trent's words when the man had implied that Kat was responsible for items disappearing from the gallery.

"*. . . Katherine's father found the stamp . . . bought it for fifteen dollars, and it was worth around fifteen thousand . . . then a few weeks after he died, it vanished.*"

TWELVE

Kat stirred, feeling a delicious sense of contentment. The sheets were warm, the pillow was comfy, James was—she opened her eyes and glanced toward his pillow . . . James was gone. As she stared, the digital clock on the nightstand went from two-twelve to two-thirteen.

Frowning, she sat up in near complete darkness, holding the sheet to her breasts. "James?" she whispered.

"I'm here." His voice came from the direction of the armchairs.

She squinted until she discerned his outline, black on black, sitting with his long legs propped on the ottoman. "Why aren't you sleeping?" she asked.

"I'm asking myself the same question," he said, his voice low and rumbling. "Considering I'm not the one who should have a guilty conscience." She heard a click, then the bulb of a small reading lamp illuminated him in a yellow haze. He had donned his slacks, but they gaped unzipped around his waist, revealing his pale underwear. He was barefoot, his legs crossed at the ankles. On the tip of his large forefinger dangled a stamp. Her father's stamp.

Her heart jumped to her throat. "Wh-What do you mean?"

His mouth tightened. "I *mean* Guy Trent told me a valuable stamp disappeared from the gallery shortly after your father was killed—he implied that you had taken it, but I didn't believe him."

She pulled the sheet higher on her chest, covering herself from his incriminating gaze. Her mind raced. Would he understand why she had taken it? He seemed to dodge emotional involvement, but if he had been close to his parents—

"Say something!" he barked, pounding his fist on the padded arm of the chair.

Kat jumped, inhaling sharply. Then anger sparked within her, and she pushed herself up and walked across the bed on her knees. "Don't you *dare* speak to me like I've done something to you! Those jackals at the gallery never gave my dad credit for anything!" Her voice and hands shook violently. Hateful, bitter words that had been festering in her stomach for years bubbled up and out of her mouth, like a cleansing regurgitation.

"For years, he begged Mr. Jellico to build a restoration center, only to be told it was a foolish idea. Then Guy Trent arrives and reads an old memo my father wrote and presented it like it was his sudden inspiration. Not only was it built, but Guy received national recognition for his innovative concept of assembly-line-style restoration teams—an idea he stole from my father's notes."

She stepped to the floor and walked closer to him, leaning forward, shaking her finger. "My father bought that stamp one day on his lunch hour—I had convinced him to leave Jellico's and he said we'd use the money to start our own antique furniture business. Instead, Guy told him he'd bought it on the gallery's time, and bullied my dad into handing it over."

To her horror, tears blurred her vision. "My dad was so naive, he just . . . handed it over." She stopped and straightened, taking a deep breath and forcing herself to calm down. "After he died, I actually forgot about it until I went into Guy's office to fetch something he was too lazy to get for himself, and there it was, laying on his desk in a mailing case, next to a sales order. The bastard had sold it for eighteen thousand dollars." Her laugh even tasted bitter on the back of her throat. "I couldn't let him do it, so I stole the stamp." She sniffed mightily. "Go ahead and call the police if you feel like you have to."

Except for his eyes, he had barely moved during her outburst. Setting her mouth, she refused to drop her gaze, refused to back down.

He pressed his lips together and held up the stamp. "So this is why you failed the polygraph?"

She nodded, wary.

"And you had nothing to do with the disappearance of the letter?"

She shook her head no.

"So why didn't you simply sell the stamp and pay off your debt to the gallery?"

"Guy would have been suspicious," she said. "Besides, just having it gives me more satisfaction than the money it would bring."

James nodded slowly, then studied the stamp for several long moments. "So," Kat said, concentrating on keeping her voice steady, "are you going to call the police?"

When James looked up, a frown carved deep lines in his face, pulling down the corners of his eyes. "I can't— I'm afraid they'll arrest me for stupidity."

His mouth twisted into a sad smile as he closed his fingers around her wrist and gently tugged her toward him. At first, Kat resisted—the fact that he was leaving today was the worst reason to succumb to him . . . and the best, she decided with a sigh, allowing herself to be pulled down on his lap. She settled into his body like floodwater searching for low ground, oozing into his crevices and leveling off.

He grabbed the end of a sheet she'd dragged onto the floor, whipped it above them with a flip of his wrists, and allowed it to float down around them. Then he clicked off the light and tucked her head beneath his neck. Relieved, spent, and a little frightened of the strong feelings coursing through her, she felt herself drifting off almost immediately, lulled by the cadence of his heart beneath her cheek.

James started awake and blinked, not sure what he'd heard. A dull sound—a distant knock perhaps? From the direction of his room came the sound of a faint scrape and a swishing noise, as if someone had slid something under his door.

He lifted his head, and winced at the needles shooting through one arm and both legs. Kat lay snuggled up against him, her breath fanning across the hair on his chest. She hadn't stirred, and he hated to wake her. The clock read only five-thirty, and her sleep had already been interrupted once.

By him—because he'd been so shaken that she'd lied to him. But even as a small part of him hoped Kat *had* lied so he'd have a reason to forget her, he'd wrung from her a soul-baring confession that triggered all kinds of protective feelings in his chest. Now as he watched her sleep, he wondered how he'd ever thought she would have committed a crime for her own personal gain. In his mind, the stamp rightfully belonged to her, and he had a new lead suspect—Guy Trent. Perhaps he and Beaman were in cahoots.

He bent his arm and made a fist, then wriggled his toes to get the blood flowing again. When he trusted his strength, he scooped her up and limped to the bed, then deposited her gently among the mussed covers, shushing her back to sleep when she stirred. A thick strand of hair had escaped the haphazard side ponytail, and as he swept it away from her face, emotion ballooned in his chest.

He'd never experienced blood-boiling lust in tandem with this intangible *thing* whose growth accompanied every thought of Katherine McKray. Whatever it was, it heightened lovemaking to near staggering proportions. But he recognized the danger in the euphoria because, like a potent drug, this *thing* gave him false confidence that he could handle obligations he knew he couldn't— mind-boggling obligations like being a husband, and a father. And the only way he had managed to survive a twenty-year career in the British Intelligence Agency was by following one commandment: Know thy limitations. It seemed like an applicable rule for civilian life too.

Clearing his head with a shake, James rubbed his eyes, then stumbled to his room in the predawn light. Indeed, a blank envelope lay on the slightly worn traffic area just inside the door. Knowing the messenger was long gone, he checked the hall anyway. Stepping back into the room, he picked up the note, then withdrew a single folded sheet of white paper. The message was printed in neat, slanted letters. *A man transacted sale of item to broker over phone; seller is reliable provider of authentic pieces; item sold to unknown third party.*

A man. Which could be a man working at the gallery—one of four security guards, including Ronald Beaman, plus Andy Wharton, Guy Trent, and two dozen or so volunteers, ticket takers, and maintenance men—or an acquaintance of a female employee. He grunted in frustration—so Kat was the only one who could be excluded.

James scanned the note again. Not much more to go on, except that the person regularly provided stolen items to the underground market. Which didn't fit Guy Trent's assertion that only a handful of items, and small-ticket items at that, had been taken from the museum over the last several months. Unless the fellow who did the brokering was being fed items smuggled from more than one gallery.

A man . . . a man. He hadn't given the Wharton guy much thought after Kat said he was harmless. Now they had more impetus to check into everyone who worked at the gallery, particularly the men. James frowned. And especially Guy Trent, whom he now thoroughly despised. Then he stopped.

Well, *they* wouldn't be checking, but Tenner would be, of course. He'd make rounds with him today to follow up on Beaman's alibi, and pass him the information from the note, then the detective could take over. What mattered most was clearing Kat's name. Finding the thief, and perhaps the letter, would simply be a bonus.

James peeked in on Kat, glad to see she was still sleeping. Having cast aside the sheet, she lay with her back to him, providing an unobstructed and tormenting view of her round derrière. His fingers twitched to touch her, but halfway to the bed he stopped and looked back to his room. He really should shower—Tenner would be expecting him to call. Then he glanced back to Kat and bit his lower lip in appreciation. Kat, Tenner, Kat, Tenner . . . he stopped. There was a decision here?

Within two seconds, he had reached the bed, then took another half second to shed his slept-in slacks and underwear. He slid in next to her warm body with his head at the foot of the bed, vice versa her position, and said good morning by covering her exquisite ankles with kisses, then traveling north from there. She roused instantly, with a surprise of her own that wrung a gasp of satisfaction from him.

From zero to sixty-nine in two and a half seconds. Even his Jaguar couldn't do that.

Kat extracted a wide gold belt from the tangled nest on her bedroom floor and turned to Denise. "Give away or throw away?"

Her friend looked up and squinted. "Hmmm. Circa nineteen eighty-eight . . . nice buckle . . . it could work."

"Good, then I'm adding it to your pile." Kat tossed it on the growing mound of clothes that were either too small or too hip for her.

"Oooh, I've never seen you wear these." Denise held up a pair of stretchy, black-and-white striped pants Kat had bought two years ago during a moment of insanity.

"I wonder why."

"Can I have them?"

"They're yours."

"Gloria has these cool shoes—" Denise stopped, then bit her bottom lip.

Kat shrugged. "Denise, it's okay. You should have told me earlier."

Her friend took a deep breath. "I didn't know how to tell you without you thinking that I've been your friend all this time because I had a crush on you or something."

Surprise and embarrassment jolted Kat, stilling her movements. "That thought hasn't entered my mind."

"Not that I don't think you're attractive," Denise said hurriedly.

Kat blinked and held up her hand. "Whoa—"

"No!" Her friend shook her head and groaned. "That's not what I meant. I think you're beautiful, Kat, but I don't find you attractive."

Frowning, Kat said, "Thanks . . . I think."

Denise threw up her hands. "Now I've really made a mess of things—which is why I didn't tell you in the first place."

"Relax," she urged her friend with a laugh. "I know what you meant. Are you going to help me sort these clothes or not?" Denise nodded and smiled.

Kat sighed in relief, glad the awkwardness had passed. She certainly had no right to pass judgment on Denise's love life, considering the fact that her own was a case study in insanity. She inspected a dress two sizes too small that still had the tags on it—inspiration for the cabbage soup diet, January 1995. "One of these days, I'm going to lose weight."

Her friend scoffed. "You've got a big bone struc-ture."

"A big bone structure? Denise, bones do not spread across the front of a chair when you sit down."

"So you've got curves—you look great." A naughty expression crossed Denise's face. "James Donovan seems to agree with me."

Kat's heart contracted. "Don't start, Denise." She'd managed to go nearly thirty seconds without thinking about him and the fact that he was leaving tonight.

"I can't believe you're not spending every minute with him until he boards that plane."

"He's spending the morning with Detective Tenner, and I had things to do here." Kat tried to force lightness into her voice. "He said he might stop by on his way to the airport."

"Well," Denise said, adopting an innocent look, "that should give you time to recover from last night—or is he a morning man?"

Kat shook her finger at her friend. "Nice try, but I neither confirm nor deny that I had relations with Mr. Donovan."

"For heaven's sake, Kat, you're walking bowlegged."

"Denise!"

"So does he wear his holster to bed?"

Kat laughed. "You're nuts."

"Oh, come on, *Pussy-Kat*, what's he like?"

Folding a T-shirt with slow, precise movements, Kat savored the images of James's lovemaking, all of them bundled tightly in her heart. She couldn't explain it, but she was afraid if she shared them with someone, the images might escape. The day would come when she would be eager to exorcise the memories, but for now, she wanted to keep them locked away. "Let's just say he's a perfect gentleman."

Denise frowned. "Oh, that's too bad. Do you think you'll see him after he leaves San Francisco?"

Kat shook her head, now accustomed to the pang of longing she felt every time she thought of the future. "No."

Denise walked over and gave Kat's shoulders a comforting squeeze. "You never know—he could show up some day with roses and a ring." She frowned in thought. "So would that make you *Mrs.* Agent James Donovan?"

Kat shook her head, smiling sadly. "Even if there were such a title, I don't think the position is available, and I'm not so sure I'd want it anyway."

"Really? God, Kat, I can tell you're crazy about the man—you wouldn't marry him?"

Pursing her lips, she struggled to put her jumbled feelings into words. "Being with James is so powerful, it's almost overwhelming, and very scary."

"Wow."

"And as G-rated as it sounds, I want a stable man who is just as crazy about me and who could see himself being a father someday."

Denise's eyes bulged. "You want kids?"

Kat pressed her lips together and nodded. "Yeah, someday. I don't want to grow old alone, Denise. I want my own family."

"Gee, Kat, you've got lots of time to think about that."

She smiled at her friend and tilted her head. "Silly, I'm not talking about next week, I'm talking about some-day. The point is, no matter how attractive, how dash-ing, or how rich the man is, I'm not sacrificing what I want, what I *need*, to play a bit part in his life. Especially since he probably goes through leading ladies like I go through Baskin-Robbins's flavor of the month."

The doorbell rang, and Kat thankfully escaped the troubling conversation, although voicing her thoughts had reinforced them in her mind. She only hoped the logical side of her brain could comfort the emotional side in the coming months.

"Who is it?" she yelled through the door as she glanced at her watch. Eleven o'clock—the locksmith was already an hour late.

"It's Guy, Kat. I need to talk to you." He sounded anxious, and contrite. "Please."

Anger barbed through her as she swung the door open. "What do you want, Guy?"

His balding head was shiny with sweat, and he swallowed nervously, then held up an envelope. "I brought your paycheck."

She snatched it out of his hand. "I was planning to pick it up when I came over this afternoon to empty my desk."

He steepled his chubby hands together. "That's what I came to talk to you about. May I come in?"

"No."

He winced. "Katherine, I'm sorry I suspended you, but you have to admit the tape was pretty convincing." She started to shut the door, but he braced it with his arm and said hurriedly, "And I figured you had a legitimate reason to get back at me."

Kat stared. "Just one reason, Guy?"

His round cheeks turned bright pink. "Well, okay, several reasons. The point is, I don't blame you for being miffed—"

"Miffed?"

"Okay, angry—furious, even. Detective Tenner called this morning to tell me the charges were dropped and said he'd be over later to question some of the employees."

"And what does this have to do with me?"

He smiled his most charming smile. "I have a proposition I believe will help you and Jellico's part on good terms."

"I don't give a rat's ass how anyone at Jellico's views my departure."

"There's a lot of money in it for you," he gasped, his jowls wiggling. "For just a few days' work." He bit his lower lip and gave her a sad face. "Please, Kat, the gallery is in chaos, and the afternoon will be shot if Tenner comes over—nothing's getting done. If you don't come back, I'm going to have to postpone the open house—which means some of the exhibits we leased just for this occasion will already be gone—which means the open house will flop—which means our attendance will be down—"

"Which means, Guy," Kat cut in, "you are in deep doo-doo."

"We need to have the open house now, while public interest is running high. With the canceled auction for the letter, I . . ." He sighed, then scratched his head. "You're right, Kat, I'm in the crapper. I just received notice that we're being audited again, and since you didn't have time to start the painting inventory, we're not going to be able to get to it before year-end. I asked Andy to step in, but no one can handle the details like you, Kat."

Unmoved, she smirked. "How much?"

He blinked. "So you would come back for a few days?"

"How much?"

Guy scratched his head. "Four thousand for two weeks?"

"Five thousand for one week and the last few hundred of my dad's so-called debt is free and clear."

"One week?"

"Actually, Friday will be my last day. I'll work extra hours until the open house Thursday evening, and by

then I'll have enough of the inventory completed to finish on Friday." She smiled. "I'll even throw in a report
for the insurance claim on the king's letter."

"*Alleged* king's letter," Guy said morosely.

"Agreed?"

He sighed. "Agreed. Can you come in this afternoon?"

Kat nodded, her smile congenial. "Draw up a contract with the terms we discussed and I'll sign it when I
get there. I'll grab my notes and come back here to make
phone calls."

He peered around her and frowned. "Are you moving?"

"Yep."

"To England?"

Her heart lurched. "What?"

He gave her a little smile. "I figured things between
you and that British fellow were heating up by now—and
frankly, I'm glad to see it." He made a regretful, clicking
noise with his roomy cheek and wrinkled his brow.
"You're a good girl, Katherine, and I'm sorry I've made
things hard for you." He shook his head. "Your dad
wasn't much of a business man, and he might have made
a few mistakes, but he was intelligent and I suppose I was
a little intimidated. In hindsight, I should have worked
with him, and I'm very sorry."

He turned and walked away. Kat closed the door and
leaned against it, tears brimming in her eyes.

"This is a nice ride," Tenner said, looking around the
Jaguar and nodding in approval. "That Lady Mercer
broad must be paying you big for this little job."

James inhaled deeply. Tenner was uncouth, but he

was predictable. "Actually, this was a personal favor for an old friend."

The detective grinned. "Is she a looker?"

Tania's face came to him, and he nodded. "I suppose so."

"Got 'em pantin' after you, don't you, son?"

James probed his cheek with his tongue, wondering how the conversation had taken such a dive. "Panting? I don't think so, no."

"Well, I don't know about this Mercer woman, but I think Ms. McKray is very nice."

"So do I," James agreed, his thoughts turning back to their morning romp.

"And I'm sorry she got dragged into this mess."

"So am I." Then he wouldn't have lost his heart to her, and wouldn't have to miss her when he left.

"Why do you think someone tried to set her up?"

James pursed his lips. "Probably to detract attention from themselves."

Tenner drummed his finger on the armrest. "Do you think it's worth our time to conduct these employee interviews?"

"*You* don't have a choice," James said. Tenner would be on his own soon. "Perhaps someone saw something. Did you discover anything interesting in the background checks?"

"Guy Trent was married several years back—to a woman from Chinatown. They have a child together."

"So he has possible connections to unload stolen goods on the Chinatown black market."

"Yep."

"What about Andy Wharton?"

"A bit of a geek, but according to his resume and

letters of reference, his work is well thought of. He doesn't strike me as being very bright, though."

Considering the source, James bit back a smile. "What about the security guards?"

"Carl Jays is the only one with a pimple—he was fired from the Fairfield art gallery across town for 'improper procedures.' I called a former co-worker who told me Carl used to show up for work, sign in, leave and go to another night watch job. Then he'd come back in time to sign out."

So the man was either extremely industrious or just plain stupid, James thought, smiling wryly. "Has he always worked for art galleries?"

Tenner twisted and reached in the backseat for the files, his breathing so labored after the effort that James regretted his question. Wheezing, the detective scanned the files, then said, "Yeah. Started right out of high school and hopped from one gallery to another for the last fifteen years."

James looked at Tenner. "Could the attraction be supplemental income from stolen art? What does he drive?"

After flipping another page or two, Tenner grunted. "A 'ninety-seven Lexus. Pretty nice car for a man who makes around thirty thousand a year." He expelled a noisy breath, whistling through his chewing gum. "I wish you would stick around, Donovan. I could sure use your help."

Feeling a tiny burst of affection for the clumsy man, James said, "Detective, I have every confidence that you will apprehend the criminal. And when you do, give him a punch for me over the trouble he caused Ms. McKray."

The detective smiled wide, snapping his gum. "You got it bad for her, don't you?"

"I'm not familiar with the term, but if you mean am I attracted—"

"Nah, son, it's more than that, ain't it?" Snap, snap. "Ever been married?"

"Er, no."

"Never been in love before, huh?"

James sighed, unwilling to discuss his private life with the man. "That's not the sort of thing I'd do."

Tenner cackled. "Son, you're in big trouble if you think it's something you can control. You can wear a bulletproof vest to protect your heart from guns and knives and such, but there ain't nothing in this world that'll keep a woman from getting in."

As Kat's face appeared in his mind, James's chest tightened and he felt the beginning of a headache in his temple. He shifted, feeling tired and itchy. If being in love felt this bad, it couldn't be good.

Tenner rubbed his chest, dislodging a belch. "Yep, ain't nothing to do but lie down and take it like a man."

THIRTEEN

"Kat!" Andy Wharton's face lit up and he clasped her in a rocking bear hug. "Thank God you're back. I told you we couldn't do the open house without you."

Guy snorted. "Andy's just glad his load will be lightened."

Andy lowered his voice as Guy walked out of hearing distance. "Napoleon is so worried about the open house, he made everyone come in over the weekend. Guy says you're going to be here through Friday?"

"Right. Just to tie up some loose ends."

"You're leaving at a good time," he said. "I hear we're being audited again and you'll be safely out of range."

Kat frowned slightly. "Out of range?"

"Well, you know how it was last time—answering questions, interruptions all the time. Besides, I'm sure it would bring back sad memories for you."

She nodded, touched by his concern. Her dad had liked working with Andy, and she was grateful for his friendship.

"Listen, Kat," he said, rubbing his hands together. "I know you always said you wouldn't date co-workers, and now that you're leaving, well . . ." His smile was shy. "I'm in L.A. occasionally—can I call you sometime?"

She suddenly realized that Andy was a cute guy, with a fresh face and large, expressive eyes. And she had always enjoyed his company. Maybe he wasn't her dream man, but he might be just the friend she needed to get over James. Her smile was wide and sincere. "I'd like that very much."

"Really? Great. That's . . . just great." He lifted his hand in a pleased wave and backed away, nodding.

Kat laughed to herself, feeling good about making plans for her new life in L.A. Her friend from college, John Cloff, said he could use her at his folk art gallery for as many hours a week as she wanted to work until she found a place to open her antique-furniture store.

Kat inhaled deeply. Things were definitely looking up—Officer Raines had even arranged for her van to be towed back to the gallery parking lot. She'd come by to pick it up, along with a copy of the contract she'd signed with Guy and her notebook of caterers, florists, musicians, and dozens of other service people who needed to be contacted with last-minute instructions before Thursday.

She grabbed her purse and turned to leave, shuddering slightly when she remembered that the last time she'd left the gallery, she'd been handcuffed. Over a single, long weekend, her life had changed so much, it was scarcely believable. She'd been arrested, freed, prompted to take an overdue step in her career, and in between, she'd managed to fall in love.

She tried to be glib about her feelings for James because it helped her deal with the hurt. People fell in love every day—she was realistic enough to know that a happy ending did not necessarily follow. Besides, James didn't feel the same way about her . . . and even if he did, it took more than love to make a relationship work. So the sooner she forgot about him, the better.

"Hallo, Pussy-Kat."

She jerked her head up, her heart jumping at the sound of his voice. He stood beside Detective Tenner, his brows knitted into one long, dark line. "What are you doing here?" she asked.

"That's odd, I was preparing to ask you the same question. Clearing your desk?"

After ordering her pulse to slow, she smiled brightly. "Not exactly—Guy needed my help for the rest of this week, and he's making it worth my while."

"I sincerely hope so," James said, his voice dubious.

"I didn't realize you were coming with Detective Tenner," Kat said. If she had, she might have taken the time to change from her old jeans and paint-splattered sweatshirt. She'd planned to simply run in and get the notebook, return home to make her business calls, take a shower, and then, like a lovestruck teenager, wait for him to drop in.

"I had a few hours to kill," he said with an easy shrug. "I was planning to stop by your place to say so long, and to see if your locks have been changed."

"Oh, um, yes, they've been changed." She squeezed the notebook to her chest and laughed cheerfully. "Now you won't have to stop by and you'll have more time to get to the airport." She'd given him an out if he wanted to take it.

He was silent for a few seconds, his eyes unreadable. "I suppose you're right."

Tenner coughed. "Want me to go ahead and get started, Donovan?"

James kept his gaze locked on her. "Sure, Detective, I'll catch up with you in a few minutes."

She watched Tenner leave, then shifted her heavy notebook to her hip.

"Why did you come back?" he asked, the anger in his voice clear.

Tiny hairs rose on the nape of her neck. She jammed her glasses higher on her nose and lifted her chin. "James, it's only for a few days and I need the money."

He strode toward her and grabbed her wrist, his eyes flashing. "I will give you the damn money to get you away from this place—how much is the little weasel paying you?"

Fury gripped her and she jerked her arm away. "I don't want your money!"

"James," came a silky voice from the doorway. "Since when do you have to get rough with your women?"

Kat turned to see what could only be described as the most gorgeous woman she'd ever seen standing with her hand on one slim hip, her perfect eyebrows in the air, her stunning gaze directed at James.

"Tania?" His eyes were wide with surprise.

"In the flesh," she said with a honeyed smile, and Kat had to agree, since so much of it was showing. She wore the briefest of minis and a loose crop top in taupe linen with a jacket to match slung over her shoulder. The bag and shoes alone probably cost more than Kat's entire wardrobe. And the flat little outie belly button . . . well, even if Kat won the lottery, that fixture was a pipe dream.

Flipping her chic, precision-cut hair, the woman

walked toward them with such smoothness, Kat wondered if her square-toed, crocodile flats were equipped with rollers. Her gaze flicked over Kat in quick dismissal. From her accent and her bearing, Kat guessed the visitor's identity, which James's flustered introduction verified.

"Katherine McKray, this is Tania Mercer."

Kat conjured up a smile and extended her hand, which still bore the slight yellowing stains of wood dye. "How do you—"

"James," Tania said, turning away, her eyes wide. "Tell me this isn't the woman who stole my letter?"

"No, Tania," he said calmly. "Kat was charged, but the charges have since been dropped."

She glanced back to Kat. "Are you quite sure she didn't do it?"

"Yes, Ms. Mercer," Kat said distinctly, dropping her hand. "I most definitely did not steal your letter."

Lady Mercer narrowed her eyes, apparently unconvinced.

"Tania," James said evenly, "what are you doing here?"

She flashed him a brilliant smile, and lay a manicured hand on his arm. "Darling, instead of meeting you in New York, I thought I would come and release you from this nonsense, then we could fly out together. Are you surprised?"

Kat gave him credit—he certainly *looked* surprised.

"I didn't realize we had decided you would join me in New York."

"Oh, James," she said with a laugh and a wave. "We really should try to *talk* more when we're together. I'm starved—let's get a bite to eat, shall we?"

Her feelings smarting, Kat began to back away quietly.

"Tania, you must not have received my message—I was planning to leave for New York tonight anyway."

She frowned beautifully. "No, I didn't. I've been pining away for you at the London cottage and decided to come straight away. Poor Mary doesn't even know I'm here."

When Kat felt safely out of range, she turned and hurried down a long hallway toward the back exit, then pushed the release bar and stepped out into the parking lot. If that's the kind of woman James wanted, then he'd probably been laughing at Kat behind her back. When she heard James call after her from the doorway, she quickly blinked away hot, absurd tears.

"Kat," he said loudly, striding up behind her and touching her forearm. "We weren't finished talking."

"Yes, James, we were."

"I don't like the notion of you coming back here—doesn't it bother you knowing the person who stole your things and planted evidence could very well be employed here, or perhaps signing your paycheck?"

She chewed on the inside of her cheek during his speech, then brushed back a wild strand of hair the wind had caught. "Sure it does, but whoever it was got what they wanted—the letter—and the charges against me have been dropped. I've been working in a near-hostile environment for years, four more days isn't going to kill me."

Kat turned to march in the direction of her dilapidated van, which had been pulled to the farthest corner of the long parking lot and left at an odd angle. Suddenly she felt a shove against her chest, as if a wall had walked into her, followed by a horrific explosion that rocked the ground where she'd been thrown facedown. Instinctively, she covered her head with her arms, and felt debris raining down around her. A piercing wail, like an unrelenting dog whistle, whined in her ears, blocking out everything else. She lay frozen, not sure what had happened, but very sure that danger was near.

Strong hands grabbed her shoulders and rolled her over, and she struck out wildly, terrified. But the hands subdued her arms and held her still. James came into focus, faded, and came back. His mouth moved and he looked angry—no, not angry, but very, very scared. She blinked hard, trying to read his lips, trying to comprehend what had happened. At last, his voice came to her in muffled syllables, still unrecognizable, but blessed confirmation that she was not deaf.

She concentrated on his wide, searching eyes, and tensed her limbs, one by one to see if they were still attached. When she realized that he was desperately trying to get her to respond to him, she nodded slowly, and his face relaxed in relief. He yelled something to someone behind him, but Kat's head felt too heavy to lift and look around.

The fact that an explosion had occurred leaked into her brain. From the gallery? A neighboring building? A gas line perhaps? Other faces appeared over hers, some distantly recognizable.

James waved everyone back, and hovered over her, stroking her hair back from her face. His hair was tousled and his impeccable clothes disheveled, which struck her as funny for some reason, and she smiled up at him. He leaned closer, tilted his head and winked at her, but his eyes were still clouded with concern.

The paramedics arrived and shuffled her onto a stretcher, then rolled her into an ambulance. She wasn't sure if James had accompanied her until she felt his hand on her socked foot. Where were her shoes?

Then they were moving and she could make out the lower pitch of the siren through the shrill hum drilling through her head. A blue-coated paramedic leaned over her and said something once, then twice, but she didn't understand him. Slowly, oh-so-slowly, sounds around her began to filter in—the bass of the ambulance engine, the muted voices of James and the paramedic talking. She grunted to see if she could hear herself, a noise that brought James and the paramedic back to her side.

"James?" she yelled—at least it sounded like a yell, except hollow and echoing. His lips moved, then his face blurred as darkness crept over her, and he slipped away.

Tenner's face was grim as he walked into the deserted waiting area where James stood fidgeting, pacing—anything to keep from screaming in frustration.

"It was a pipe bomb, wasn't it?" James asked from across the room.

The detective nodded and expelled a noisy breath, dragging his hand through his sparse hair. "How's Ms. McKray?"

"Lots of cuts and bruises, and her ears will ring for a few days, but the doctors say she'll be fine." James massaged his neck, then rolled his shoulder.

"How about you?" Tenner asked. "Looks like you got nicked yourself."

James touched the small bandage at his temple and scoffed. "It's just a scratch—I let them dress it to be near Kat."

"What the devil happened?"

The fury and helplessness he'd managed to hold at

bay ballooned in his chest, threatening to break him apart. James snapped and spun toward Tenner. "Bloody hell, man, she was almost killed right in front of me, that's what happened!" Then he turned and slammed his hand into the wall and leaned against it as the blessed, comforting pain subsided.

He heard the detective walk closer, then the creak of a chair being filled with a big body. "Won't do her no good if you go bustin' up yourself, son."

James closed his eyes, then sighed and slowly turned around, massaging his knuckles. "I did that for myself, not for Kat."

"I need to file a report," Tenner said gruffly.

Lowering himself into a vinyl seat across from Tenner, James nodded.

"A woman called a local newspaper and claimed responsibility for the bomb," the detective said.

Astonishment washed over him. "What?"

"The guy said she sounded Asian—maybe Chinese. Some rambling message about abortion clinics—there's been a rash of small bombings lately . . . no fatalities yet, though."

James frowned in confusion. "This was some kind of random political statement?"

Tenner frowned. "In my opinion, no. I'd say someone wanted to kill Ms. McKray and made the phone call to throw us off, or some nut took it upon herself to claim the bombing. Now, tell me what happened."

James took a deep breath and leaned forward, resting his elbows on his thighs, and repeated every detail he could recall from the time Tenner had left them alone in the gallery to the time of the explosion.

"Did you see anyone hanging around the parking lot?"

"No."

"How about anyone pulling away in a vehicle when you came outside?"

"No."

Tenner grunted. "You're both damned lucky, if you ask me."

"How could someone plant a bomb in her van—wasn't it searched when they towed it in?"

"Yep, clean as a whistle."

"How about before it was towed back?"

"Can't be sure, but anyone who would sneak into a police impound lot and plant a pipe bomb has got gonads the size of my bowling ball."

"So your guess would be that the bomb was planted after the van was returned to the gallery?"

"That'd be my guess."

"Has the area been sealed and everyone questioned?"

Tenner nodded. "Yep, but now the case has been handed over to the bomb squad, and the FBI will probably step in. My car, along with every other car on the lot, has been confiscated for evidence." He exhaled, puffing out his cheeks. "I'm just glad this isn't a murder investigation. When I heard that boom, I nearly pissed my pants."

James lifted his head and smiled, appreciating the man's attempt to lighten the mood for a moment before he turned serious again. "Why would someone want to kill her, Tenner? The charges had been dropped, so the police were already looking elsewhere for a suspect. What could possibly be gained from getting rid of her?"

The detective sighed and scratched his belly. "That's a good question."

Watching him squirm, James knew the man was holding back a theory. His heart skipped. "What is it,

Tenner? Is she involved in this somehow—have I missed something because I'm . . . because I'm too close?"

Frowning, Tenner grimaced. "I don't know, Donovan, but there's only one reason to get rid of her—she knows something she hasn't told."

James pursed his lips, his mind racing. "Or she knows something she doesn't realize is important."

"Right," Tenner said, leaning forward. "And it's our job to find out what it is."

"Were you able to uncover anything concrete from the background checks we discussed?"

"It was payday, so Carl Jays had come by the gallery to pick up his check. His Lexus was in the parking lot at the time of the bombing, too, but carrying a higher-priced cargo than most of the cars."

"Drugs?"

"Yep. Did all his dealing at night—working midnight shifts at art galleries was the perfect cover."

"So we're down one suspect."

"Looks that way."

"Mr. Donovan?" a nurse asked as she walked in with a chart.

He jumped to his feet. "Yes?"

"Ms. McKray is ready to go. Will you sign her out and be responsible for her?"

To James, the question touched something deep inside him. The idea of not being responsible for Katherine was unthinkable, and a revelation that would have to wait for closer scrutiny. "I will," he said, reaching for the papers.

"I can walk," Kat protested when James swung her into his arms.

"I know, but it gives me an excuse to put my hands on you," he whispered close to her ear.

She smiled, secretly glad to be carried into her apartment. Her face and arms felt tight from many tiny cuts, and she was still a little light-headed. Tenner had driven them to her apartment in his newly acquired squad car, and brought up the rear carrying James's suitcase and the figurine boxes.

"Are you staying?" she asked, her eyebrows lifted.

His nod brooked no argument. "And Officer Raines was so shaken up, I believe he's going to keep an eye on things outside."

As he set her down on the couch, Kat looked around and frowned. "It was a mess in here before, but something is different." She caught James's and Tenner's exchanged glances. "What?" She reached up to poke James in the shoulder. "Tell me!"

He lowered himself to sit next to her on the sofa. "The police swept your place before we brought you home."

She felt the blood drain from her face. "You mean for another bomb?"

He nodded, his face drawn.

Fear and frustration clogged her throat. "Why is this happening to me?"

"That's what we intend to find out," Tenner said, moving a straight-back chair closer to the couch. "Let's say for the time being this wasn't a political statement and assume it had something to do with the gallery break-in. Agent Donovan and I think that whoever is after you thinks you know something incriminating about them."

She frowned. "But if I did, I would've already reported it."

"Would you?" James asked with a pointed look.

"Of course."

"What about Guy Trent's attempt to extort you? You didn't report that."

Kat looked quickly at Tenner, and James said, "I filled him in."

Frowning, she said, "That's different—I didn't have to pay back the money. I had a choice, but I agreed to it anyway. Technically, that's not really extortion, is it?"

Tenner pressed his lips together then said, "Technically, no. Companies often offer employees a payback schedule to avoid prosecution for theft—the publicity really isn't good for them or the employee, so everyone is happy."

"Think, Kat," James said, taking her hand. His touch never failed to set her heart to fluttering, even when the mood was so serious. "Are you absolutely sure you don't know anything that would be damaging to someone at the gallery? Something that no one else would know?"

Her mind raced backward and forward, trying to seize some minute detail that had escaped her in its simplicity, but she shook her head. "No."

Tenner folded a stick of gum into his mouth. "Maybe walk in a room on the tail end of a conversation, or pick up a phone and overhear something?"

"No, not that I can remember." She touched a hand to the base of her skull where it had started to pound.

"Maybe we better wait until tomorrow to finish this," James said, nodding to Tenner, who stood and hitched up his pants.

"Okay, I'll see you all in the morning. Try to get some rest, Ms. McKray."

James closed the door and turned the deadbolts, then walked back to the couch. "Want to lie down?"

She nodded, then slid down and drew up her legs, leaving room for him to sit on the end. He did, but he pulled her feet into his lap, straightening her legs into a more comfortable position.

"I should thank you," she said, glancing at him through her lashes. "Lately every time I look up, there you are."

He smiled and lay his head back, massaging her feet. "It's my job."

Disappointment rose in her chest. Still the dutiful agent. "Shouldn't you be on your way to the airport?"

He rolled his head toward her. "New York will still be there."

"And where is Lady Mercer?" Kat acquired a mock accent and lifted her nose in the air.

James grunted and expelled a short breath. "I believe she checked into the Flagiron." He grinned and leaned toward her. "Careful, Pussy-Kat, if I didn't know better, I might think you were jealous."

"I'm still delirious from the blast."

His thumbs were working magic on her insteps. "Believe me, you have nothing to be jealous of where Tania is concerned."

"She's very beautiful."

"Yes."

"And slender."

"Again, yes."

"And rich."

"Three for three," he said with a smile.

"Nice?"

He squinted. "It depends, but today, no."

"So," she said, studying her cuticles. "Do you two have an understanding?"

"If you mean that Tania and I understand there is nothing between us, then yes."

"But you were lovers."

He dropped his gaze, but nodded, still rubbing her feet.

Well, it was certainly hard to blame the woman for staking her claim, Kat acknowledged with a little barb of remorse. After all, he had slept in Tania's bed long before he'd slept in hers.

"I didn't ask, Kat," he said softly, "but I assumed you weren't a virgin either."

She smiled wryly. "No."

A slow grin spread across his face. "Good, because if I had despoiled you, I would have felt a gentlemanly obligation to marry you."

Her heart cartwheeled over the mere mention of the word, but she kept an innocent, light smile on her face. "Horror of horrors."

His gaze was steady, but unreadable. "I'm glad we see eye to eye on some things, Pussy-Kat." Giving her feet a final pat, he slid out from under them and said, "I'll get your bed ready and come back for you."

"No, I'll walk," Kat insisted, swinging her feet to the floor, and standing up slowly. He took her arm and they headed into her room, then Kat diverted to the bathroom. She frowned at the abrasions on her face and arms, but thanked her guardian angel for the hundredth time for keeping her and James safe.

The thought of their most recent conversation resurrected the hurt in her chest. James couldn't have made it more clear that if he had intentions of settling down, it wouldn't be soon, and it wouldn't be with her. Yet she had to admire his honesty in this age of cat-and-mouse games. And ironically, if anything, it made her feelings toward him even stronger. She gingerly pulled a night-gown over her head, then shuffled back into the bed-room.

She hadn't realized how sleepy she was until she felt the mattress at her back. James extinguished all the lights but a small lamp, then removed his shirt and shoulder holster. He checked his gun and laid it on the night-stand, then piled extra pillows next to her and sat against the headboard on top of the covers, his legs stretched out in front of him.

Kat closed her eyes and tried to forget about the man next to her. She dozed fitfully, then awakened around two o'clock, her mind working feverishly. She was on the verge of remembering something, she could feel it. She focused on James's deep, even breathing, the rise and fall of his chest in the dim lamplight, hoping her subcon-scious would take over. Suddenly, a thought struck and she reached over to shake James's shoulder before it es-caped her. He jerked awake, his eyes wide, his hand au-tomatically going to his gun on the nightstand. "What? Are you all right?"

"Don't shoot," she said, only half joking. "I just thought of something."

He sagged against the headboard in relief, then leaned forward to stretch his lower back. "What?"

"James, what if it's not something I've *already* seen or heard, but something I would have encountered in the near future?"

He frowned, then launched a full-body stretch, punc-tuated with a shuddering yawn. "You mean like some-thing at the open house?"

"Possibly. Maybe someone I would have met?"

He nodded. "Someone who might discuss something with you, either purposefully or in innocence."

She shrugged. "Too far-fetched?"

Scrubbing his hands over his face, he shook his head. "Maybe not. Is anything else going on right now, something internal to the gallery?"

"Well, there's the audit, but Guy approves all expenditures, so no one would have a reason to do something behind my back, like forge my signature."

"Do you approve selling prices?"

"Yes."

"Could someone be skimming?"

"It's possible, I suppose, but they would have to dispose of Guy, too, since he countersigns the sales slips."

"Unless it's Guy who's doing the skimming."

His eyes were still closed, but she knew he was awake. "But then why rehire me—I was ready to walk away."

"But the auditors would subpoena you no matter where you went."

She shuddered. Could she have worked for a man all these years who would commit a cold-blooded murder?

He inhaled deeply, then blinked wide, obviously trying to concentrate in spite of his exhaustion. Kat felt a rush of appreciation—and love—for him. Every woman should be so blessed as to have a brush with a real, live hero, she decided.

"What about something you do as a regular part of your job?" he asked. "Something no one else does?"

She frowned and started to shake her head, then stopped. "Well . . . there is one thing," she said slowly.

He opened his eyes and turned his head toward her. "What?"

"The painting vaults are inventoried every three years. . . . I was just getting started last Friday."

He sat up straight. "And the burglary interrupted you."

"Right." Then her eyes widened. "James—one of the reasons Guy hired me back was to finish the inventory."

FOURTEEN

"It's that artsy-fartsy, long-haired Wharton guy, ain't it?" Tenner's voice barked over the phone.

"So it would seem," James said, trying to summon the elusive thought that kept nagging the base of his brain. He shifted the receiver uncomfortably, tired and keyed up at the same time. "My guess is he's creating forgeries and storing them in the vault, then selling the originals."

"And Ms. McKray was on the verge of finding them when she started the inventory, so he framed her for the break-in to get her out of the way?"

"Right."

"Hmmm—guess he wasn't as dense as I thought. How's he been smuggling in the fakes?"

"According to Kat, Andy supervised the construction of the restoration center based on her father's hand-drawn plans. My guess is he had a secret closet built in and that's where he's doing the work."

"Damn—right inside the place. Want me to pick up Wharton?"

James glanced at his watch. "No. Send someone else to arrest Wharton, and send an officer to stay with Kat. Then meet me at the gallery in forty-five minutes." He depressed the button, disconnecting Tenner, his mind racing. Then he slowly dialed a London number. "Bernard, it's James Donovan. I'm in the States, and I need your help. . . . Yes, anything to connect the name Andrew Wharton with the Webster art gallery in London." He spelled the last name. "I'll be at this number in San Francisco for the next thirty minutes."

"I just can't believe it." Wrapped in a robe and sporting her fuzzy house shoes, Kat stood in the kitchen, shaking her head. "I thought Andy was a friend of my father's . . . a friend of mine."

"Don't blame yourself," James said softly, pulling himself to his feet. "Some people only show you the side they want you to see." He tingled, feeling like a hypocrite, considering that was how he had behaved around Kat, afraid to let her see how deeply he cared about her.

His heart filled at the sight of the abrasions on her body—she'd nearly been killed for the sake of someone's greed. The thought flashed through his mind that he'd been given a wake-up call: seize the opportunity to plan a future with Katherine. But the old concerns were still there. Could he move in and out of the daily routine of being a husband for the next forty years with a smile on his face and sincerity in his heart? Did he have the strength to relinquish control over some parts of his life? He'd been completely independent of other people for so long, he simply didn't think he could incorporate them into his life at this late date.

"I made some coffee," she said, pushing a mug toward him.

"Thanks," he said, striding forward to take a great,

hot gulp, then turned back to her bedroom. "I'm waiting for a phone call, then I'm meeting Tenner at the gallery."

"I heard." She followed him into the bedroom, and when he shrugged into his shirt, he noticed she was disrobing. Even the brevity of the moment could not prevent his body from reacting when she pulled her short gown over her head.

"Pussy-Kat," he said with a low laugh, unable to take his gaze from her bare breasts, "although I'd like nothing better than to usher in the dawn pleasuring each other, perhaps now isn't the time—"

"I'm going with you," she said, donning a T-shirt, then a sweatshirt.

His expression changed abruptly. "No, you are not."

She stepped into a pair of jeans and quickly pulled them up over her hips, then fixed him with a hard stare. "Yes, I am. I'm the one who was framed for the break-in, I'm the one who was arrested, and I'm the one who was targeted for that bomb—I'm going with you. I might just be able to help you two find what you're looking for. Besides," she added with a wry smile, "do you trust my safety to a police officer standing watch at my door, or would you rather me be with you?"

He scowled and finished dressing in silence, unable to argue with her logic, but unwilling to acquiesce verbally. As she brushed her hair and pulled it back into a low ponytail, he saw that she moved gingerly and winced a time or two. She was stubborn. A taste of what it would be like to live with her, he noted wryly.

The phone rang just as he finished washing and toweling his face. "James Donovan here. . . . Yes, hello, Bernard, do you have something for me? . . . Oh? . . . Just as I suspected, I'm afraid. . . . Yes, let the London police know that the Wharton fellow is probably being arrested as we speak. . . . I'll call you later, old man, thanks for your assistance."

Kat's eyes bulged. "Andy is connected to forgeries at a London gallery?"

He nodded grimly. "His name has come up, along with others. Didn't you say he studied art in Europe?"

"Yes."

"Well, he obviously developed long-lasting friendships with the wrong sort of people."

A knock on the door interrupted them, and Officer Campbell announced that Tenner had sent him. James admitted him and explained the change in circumstances, glaring at Kat. Officer Campbell offered them a ride, and James accepted, since he had planned on walking to meet Tenner before having Kat's company forced upon him.

The detective sat waiting in his "new" car when they arrived. Remnants of yellow police crime scene tape dangled from low cement pillars in the parking lot.

Tenner climbed out of the clunker, his gum snapping with intensity. "What's she doing here?"

James frowned. "Weren't you the one spouting advice the other day about women?"

"Just because I live with four of 'em don't make me no expert," Tenner grumbled.

Kat stepped between them. "At least the gallery was spared from the blast."

"Good thing there was no glass on this side," remarked the detective.

She looked around, expecting to feel fear or dread, but the area seemed innocently normal. She noticed two cars parked out where her van had been yesterday, one that she knew belonged to Ronald Beaman and the other to a female guard she knew as Nisa. She shuddered to think that a few parked cars between her and the van had probably spared her life.

A hand-lettered sign on the door read "Will reopen Friday." So Guy had finally conceded to defeat, she noticed. The open house must have been canceled. Unfortunately, he had no idea of the scandal that would shake the gallery to its foundation in the days to come. James pounded on the back door and waved to the camera pointed at them. Within a few minutes, Ron Beaman came to the door, his eyes wide. "Is something wrong?"

"We need to come in and take a look around the restoration center," Tenner said, flashing his badge unnecessarily.

The security guard bit his bottom lip, and Kat tried to force her thoughts from the costume in which she'd last seen him. "I'm not sure about this," Ronald said. "I'm going to have to call Mr. Trent."

"Go call him," the detective said casually. "But this is still considered the scene of at least one crime, so I don't have to have your permission, I was just being nice." In a burst of power that surprised Kat, he pushed his way in, and she and James followed.

"Is anyone else in the building?" James asked.

Ronald's eyes moved around nervously. "Just me and Nisa, the other guard."

They moved down the hall as a unit, then into the new wing with Kat leading the way, her heart pounding in anticipation.

"Open it," James ordered Beaman. The man jangled a huge set of metal card readers on a chain, finally finding the right one and swinging open the door.

"I need to get back to my rounds," Ronald said, backing away from them.

"We'll take it from here," James assured him.

Kat walked in first, turning on lights as she went and looking around the sterile room, which resembled a medical lab. Looking for what, she didn't know.

"Give us a brief tour," James said, his gaze sweeping the room, missing nothing, she was sure. She showed him each of the four large rooms, including a tiled area with aluminum fixtures and a long, narrow storage room lined with containers of all kinds—cleaners, paints, turpentine.

"We've circled back around, haven't we?" James asked, almost to himself, his head pivoting as he walked.

Kat looked around to gain her bearings. "You're right—on the other side of that wall, no, *that* wall"—she pointed to the row of supply-laden cabinets—"is the painting vault."

James and Tenner moved deeper into the supply room and headed for the short wall on the end at the same time. The men exchanged glances, then both started pulling supplies from the floor-to-ceiling metal shelves.

"Well, what do you know," Tenner said. He swung out an emptied section of shelving that was hinged to the wall, revealing a sliding panel the size of a three-drawer file cabinet.

"I'm afraid I'll have to stop you right there," a menacing voice called from behind them.

James froze, then turned around slowly to see Andy Wharton standing beside Kat, holding a pistol up and out at shoulder level, aimed directly at her left ear. His heart jumped to his throat, and he drew blood from his tongue.

"Wait a minute, Wharton," Tenner said, raising his arm slowly. "Forgery and burglary will only get you a few months—murder is another matter altogether."

"Then I guess I just blew it," Andy said, his mouth twisting into a grin. "Because Beaman is lying in the hall with a bullet through his head." He laughed. "I insisted on maximum soundproofing when these walls were built."

"And the other guard?" James asked.

"She's tied up, but she'll die in the fire."

"The fire?" he pressed, trying to stall.

"Oh, yeah," Andy said with confidence. "This whole place has to go. Does anyone have something to start a fire with?" He glanced at the shelves packed with flammable solvents and laughed hysterically.

James saw that Kat had started to shake, her gaze darting sideways, then back to him. He nodded to her, trying to comfort her with his eyes and hide the fact that he himself was shaking inside. He'd nearly watched her die yesterday—he wasn't about to watch her be executed today.

He jerked his head to indicate the panel they'd uncovered. "Soundproof walls—so you could work undetected in your little lab?" he asked, his voice unbelievably casual.

"Yeah," Andy said with pride in his voice.

"And I suppose there's also a hidden door to the vault in your lab."

"Uh-huh. I could take things out for hours at a time and no one knew, no one even suspected. Ingenious, wasn't it?"

"You're right, Mr. Wharton," James said agreeably. "We quite underestimated you. I have to admit, you fooled many people for a rather long time. Except perhaps for Mr. McKray." He saw Kat's eyes close and prayed she wouldn't faint. Wharton looked so wild-eyed, he might shoot at the first movement.

The man frowned, and his hand dropped an inch. "Frank was starting to get in the way, being a little too nosy for his own good, so I fixed his brakes."

James nodded sympathetically. "He found out you were behind the embezzling—I suppose you needed start-up funds?"

Andy pursed his lips. "Someone told me you were smart."

Conjuring up his most charming smile, James moved his hands to his waist. His gun was at his back, beneath his jacket, but he wasn't going to risk any quick movements. "Which brings me to another point," James said, shaking his head. "How you were able to branch out internationally—I'm dying to meet your London connection."

Andy's grin was slow and sweet. "Are you now?"

"Tania," James called, "you might as well show yourself."

After a few seconds of silence, he heard the sound of a woman's heels clicking on the tiled floor in the other room. Tania appeared, dressed in a black pantsuit and boots, her hair tucked beneath a black beret, holding a box of long matches. "James, darling, I hate to see it come to this."

James smiled sadly. "You wanted me out of England because you knew they had asked me to work on the Webster museum case in London."

She raised her lovely hands in a shrug. "You're the best—I knew you would find me out."

"So you shipped me here with a fake love letter."

Tania sighed. "Very fake. You were supposed to be gone by the time the burglary took place—but you missed your damn plane." She frowned in Kat's direction. "I wonder what could have distracted you. Women have always been your weakness, James. I'm afraid this little dalliance will cost you your life."

"You beat me to San Francisco, didn't you?" he asked. "It was you on the videotape, stealing the letter."

She nodded, her eyes alight with drama. "Andy knew she was going to stumble across the forgeries when she inventoried the vault, so we came up with a way to get her out from underfoot." Her lip curled in disgust. "But your libido got in the way and messed up our entire plan."

"And you planted the bomb," he said, masking his anger. "I never figured you for a killer, Tania."

"It's your fault—you forced our hand."

"Surely you can't imagine you'll get away with this."

"We have enough money now to buy new identities."

His eyes flicked to the scrawny Wharton, whose arm was shaking from holding the gun. "And this is the man with whom you're going to spend your life as a fugitive?" He didn't attempt to keep the disdain from his voice.

Andy swung his face toward Tania, but she only narrowed her eyes. "Let's just say there's more to him than meets the eye, James."

James smirked, and scratched his rib cage. "Ah, so your well-endowed painter boyfriend knows how you convinced me to make this trip?"

Her smile faltered, and Andy's brow crumpled in confusion. "What? You were on your back with him?"

James shook his head. "Oh, no, Wharton, Tania's positions were much more creative than that."

"What?" Wharton screamed, swinging his gun forward and away from Kat's head. James jerked his gun out of his waistband and fired two shots in succession, hitting the man in the shoulder both times. Kat screamed and slammed against the cabinet behind her. Wharton fell back, firing his gun, and James heard Tenner grunt in pain. He looked back to see the detective lying on his back in a pool of blood, his eyes open and darting side to side.

"Tenner!" Kat gasped and lunged for him.

Tania grabbed the gun and yanked Wharton to his feet. She aimed at James and shot wildly, ricocheting two bullets off the tiled floor. James dove for her legs and knocked her off her feet, the impact sending both weapons skittering across the floor. Tania fought like a wildcat, kicking, biting, and clawing. James knocked her out cold with one right jab. "Sorry, old gal," he whispered, then let her fall back to the floor.

"James, look out!" Kat screamed.

He rolled over and saw Wharton towering over him with the gun aimed at his chest. The man's face glistened with sweat, his shoulder oozed blood in two places. His eyes were slightly glazed, and his lip curled back in a sneer. His finger started to squeeze the trigger. "Ugghh!" His eyes bulged in outraged pain as he froze for two seconds, then fell sideways, discharging the gun as he dropped.

James ducked, feeling a zinging vibration between his legs as the bullet struck too close for comfort. When he lifted his head, Kat stood, still holding the glass canister she'd bashed into Wharton's head.

"Varnish," she said with a shaky smile.

"I'll add it to my arsenal. How's Tenner?"

"He's conscious—I'll call nine one one."

FIFTEEN

James knocked on the open door and stuck his head into the hospital room. "Are you up to the task of talking?"

"Well, if it isn't Agent Donovan." Tenner gave him a face-splitting grin from the hospital bed. "Sure, come on in. What did you bring me?"

James handed him a greasy sack with a wry smile. "Italian sausage with mustard and onions, and cheese fries with chili on the side."

Tenner beamed. "Thank you, Donovan, you really know how to make a man happy."

He cocked an eyebrow. "Well, I must say, that's the first time anyone has ever told me that. How are you feeling?"

Tenner tore into the sack and stuffed a fry into his mouth. Then he patted his stomach, bulging under the thin hospital gown. "Just a flesh wound, and thank goodness I have plenty of that. I should be out in plenty of time for the trial. How's Beaman?"

James frowned. "Not as cheerful as you, old chap, but he'll pull through. I've come to say good-bye."

The detective's brow furrowed. "You're leaving?"

He nodded.

"Taking Ms. McKray with you, I hope."

James lowered his gaze. He hadn't been able to shake the chest-tightening blahs since he rolled off Kat's couch this morning. Between her healing injuries and mutual wariness, they had silently agreed on separate sleeping arrangements for the last two nights.

"Er, no," he said. "I'm due in New York tonight and Kat is leaving for L.A. next week to start a business with an unexpected windfall from Guy Trent."

"Oh?"

"When he discovered that Wharton had been behind the embezzling, he gave back the money she'd paid for her father's debt—with interest."

Tenner's mouth pulled upward. "That's great for the missy. Wharton's been charged?"

James nodded. "Tania turned on Wharton. Now he'll be tried for murdering Kat's father in addition to all the other charges."

"What'll happen to the Mercer woman?"

"She agreed to a plea bargain here, but she'll still have to stand trial in London. She might see the light of day in a few years, but she'll be broke and shamed—not quite the exotic adventure she'd planned for herself."

"No, life doesn't always turn out the way we plan, does it, Agent Donovan?"

James knew what the man was hinting at, but didn't rise to the bait. "No, it doesn't, but it always seems to turn out for the best, doesn't it?"

Tenner gave him a crooked smile. "I'm going to be a father again."

Surprise shot through him. "Really? So she did it with you again?"

"What?"

James shook his head. "I mean, she did it *to* you again." He laughed weakly. "My, my."

"Yeah, a baby at my age—don't that beat all?" Tenner belly-laughed, winced and clutched his stomach, then smiled. "Hope it's another girl."

"Then I do too," James said, extending his hand. "Good luck, Detective. I hope you get home to your womenfolk soon."

"Agent Donovan," Tenner said, his eyes bright, "it's been a pleasure working with you. Glad I could introduce you to the finer foods of this good country."

Looking down at the grease shining on his hand from Tenner's slippery grip, he simply inclined his head with a smile.

"Too bad I couldn't teach you more about women," he said as James walked to the door.

"Thank you, Detective, but I've made it this far on my own rather well in that category."

"You're running, son."

James glanced back at the man and pointed to his watch. "Running late. Good-bye, Detective." But his steps slowed as he walked down the hall. His good-bye to Kat would be torturous for him—why was he rushing to prolong it? If he timed it just right, it would be fast, clean, painless. Or at least less painful.

As Kat folded towels from the dryer, she packed them in a box labeled "Bathroom Linens" and glanced out the window for the fiftieth time. He had to come back before he went to the airport—he'd left his luggage and his figurines. She sighed. And his smell, and his laugh.

Tears, which had hovered near the surface all day, pricked her eyelids, but she widened her eyes and blinked them away, forcing herself to smile.

She just wanted to get it over with, to say good-bye and watch him walk away so she could start getting over him, so she could begin her new life in L.A. with a clean slate. She loved him, and she knew he cared about her, too, even though "love wasn't in his vocabulary." For her, it was simply a case of right person, wrong time. They wanted different things out of life: She wanted marriage, a home, and a family, and he wanted . . . well, she wasn't sure what James wanted, she just knew his plans didn't include the words "monogamy" and "daddy."

Kat checked her watch again—he had to leave for the airport in thirty minutes to make it on time. Denise was coming over later for a good old-fashioned breakup pizza party, a prelude to the farewell pizza party planned for next week.

She truly was looking forward to leaving the city— she had too many sad memories here, especially after the showdown with Andy Wharton and Tania Mercer. Just thinking about it sent shudders through her: Had James not stayed in San Francisco, she'd either be in jail or dead. She owed him her life, and knew the gift she had for him was only a token, but she felt like she needed to do something. Plus some part of her wanted him to have something that would remind him of her. She smirked— something besides powder burns on his thighs from the shot Wharton had fired as he passed out from her direct hit.

Twenty-five minutes later she'd decided he had forgone their good-bye and would probably send a courier, James Donovan style, to pick up his luggage and ship it.

A huge lump formed in her throat when she realized that he hadn't wanted to see her again. She actually thought they had shared a special bond. Instead he was probably already thinking ahead to the next adventure.

The knock on her door sent her pulse jumping and she smoothed a hand over her loose hair as she walked to the door. When she opened the door, he was holding onto the door frame, smiling like the devil's evil brother. "Hallo, Pussy-Kat." Then he glanced at her slacks and blouse. "I was hoping you'd be naked."

She made a good attempt at a smile, she thought. While she was wallowing in angst wondering how she was going to say good-bye, he was as breezy as a kite, just flying through, ma'am.

He leaned forward to give her a light, swift kiss, then glanced at his watch. "Not much time for good-byes, Pussy-Kat, I've got a plane to catch."

She nodded, biting her lower lip. Disappointment sawed through her—she hated that their parting was going to be so . . . so . . . so common. But it only reinforced her earlier assessment that her feelings obviously ran deeper than his.

He nodded to the Woman box. "I'm leaving you the female figurine, so take good care of her."

Kat frowned, shaking her head. "James, I can't accept a gift like that—it's much too expensive and it means—"

"It means nothing," he said curtly, his tone cutting her deep. He sighed, raking his hand through his hair. "I simply decided I don't have room for both pieces, and I don't feel like lugging the pair all the way to New York."

She blinked and swallowed and forbade herself to cry.

His mouth was set in a firm line. "It doesn't represent something larger, if that's what you're worried about. If you don't want to be bothered with it either, take it back to the dealer and see if he'll take it off your hands."

Kat bit her tongue, determined not to let him see how much he was hurting her. "Okay," she said softly.

He had gathered up his suitcase and the Man box and was backing out the door when she remembered the gift. She reached for the small package and fingered the paper she'd so carefully wrapped around it. "Um, James."

His brow was still furrowed when he glanced up, and climbed in surprise when he spotted the gift.

She shrugged. "Just a little something to say thank you."

James stopped, then looked flustered. "My cab's waiting—"

"Go," she said, shooing him out the door and smiling as wide as she dared. "You can open it later—it, um, doesn't represent something larger."

He straightened and looked at her, and when she felt composed, she lifted her gaze to his. "See you in the movies," she quipped.

One dimple appeared. "Pardon?"

She shook her head and whispered, "Private joke."

"Good-bye, Pussy-Kat, I hope you find everything your heart desires in the City of Angels."

Her heart twisted—she could almost feel it cracking open. "Good-bye, Agent Donovan, I wish the same for you in your worldly travels."

He flashed both dimples, and then he was gone.

Kat resisted the urge to watch him walk away. She simply closed the door and slid down it until she sat on the bare wood floor, her tears falling freely.

❖━━━❖

James cleared his throat for the tenth time to dislodge the clump of emotion he felt at leaving Kat. In his bumbling attempt to avoid a sappy good-bye, he'd hurt her feelings. What a cad he'd been.

"Got a cold?" the cabbie asked conversationally.

"Er, yes . . . I believe I am coming down with something."

"Sounds bad."

James glanced down at the wrapped package in his lap. "It is, it's quite bad, actually."

"Drink lots of fluids," the fellow said.

"Do martinis count?" James asked with a wry grin.

"Hell, yeah." The man pointed at the package. "Whatcha got there?"

"I'm not sure—it's a gift."

"Aren't you gonna open it?"

James nodded, then carefully tore the ends loose. He tore away several layers until he withdrew a fat leather case, from which protruded a copper-colored metal tube with a decorative screw-top lid.

"What is it?" the guy asked.

"It's a portable humidor," James said, his heart doing strange things inside his tight chest.

"For cigars?"

"Yes."

"Wow, it looks nice."

"Indeed," James replied, alternately caressing the metal and the leather. The initials JD had been engraved in simple block letters on the lid.

"From a girlfriend?"

James frowned. "Not really." He looked back to the gift and smiled. "Just a wonderful lady I met during my visit." He carefully unscrewed the lid and blinked as the strong aroma of tobacco filled his nostrils.

"Did she put a cigar in it too?"

James pinched the top of the cigar, his heart thudding as he withdrew it from the metal cylinder. "Bloody hell," he whispered.

"Must be a good one."

"The best," James agreed softly, studying one of the Cuban cigars that had been her father's. Her most precious treasure, and she'd given one to him.

"No, Denise, really I'm fine," Kat said into the phone. "I just don't feel like getting together tonight, that's all. . . . No, I think the excitement of the last few days is catching up with me. . . . Yeah, thanks, I'll call you tomorrow."

When she hung up, she stared morosely at the Woman package. With a sigh, she slit open the box and lifted the heavily wrapped figurine. She carefully tore away the layers until she uncovered the jade female, translucent, resplendent . . . and alone. She felt a brief pang for the woman, who might never be reunited with her true partner. Then she smiled sadly—she was commiserating with a statue. "Want some ice cream?" she asked Woman.

What hurt the most was that she had so misjudged his affection for her. All along it had been a convenient, physical relationship, and nothing more.

She poured herself a glass of wine, with two scoops of vanilla ice cream on the side, then turned on the stereo and wrapped another cabinet of dishes in a stack of newspapers. She'd started on a second cabinet when she heard a knock at the door. Kat smiled—how would she make it in L.A. without Denise?

Wiping her newsprint-stained hands on a paper

towel, she padded to the door and swung it open, grinning. Then her grin dissolved.

"Hallo, Pussy-Kat." James's voice was low and his smile seemed a bit strained. His suitcase and Man squatted on the floor next to his feet.

Her throat constricted, and the first thing that went through her mind was that she couldn't handle another good-bye. "Did you miss your plane?"

"I'm afraid so."

"Traffic?"

"No. I love you."

Kat blinked, and her heart vaulted. "Excuse me?" she whispered.

His brow crumpled. "Didn't I say it properly? I practiced all the way back from the airport. The cabbie said I had it down rather nicely. I love you."

She checked her impulse to rush into his arms, remembering all the reasons their relationship wouldn't work. "It's not that simple, James."

His shoulders fell. "You don't love me?" He turned a full circle, then looked down at Man and scoffed. "I've made a bloody fool of myself, haven't I?"

"James," she said hurriedly, trying not to smile and water down this very tense moment, "the fact of the matter is, I do love you."

"Is this where you say we can be friends, because the cabbie told me to watch out for that one."

She pressed her lips together, then tried again. "No, James, I'm not trying to give you the brush-off, I really do love you."

He smiled and opened his mouth, then bit his bottom lip and held up his hands. "Kat, help me here, I'm dying. This is the first time in my life I've ever told a woman that I love her and I don't know where to go from here. What do you mean 'it's not that simple'? I love you, you love me—"

"James, I want marriage—"

"We'll have one—"

"And a home—"

"We'll have two—"

"And children—"

"We'll have three!" He picked her up and spun her around. "Please say yes, Pussy-Kat." He let her slide down his body, coming to rest face to face with him. He leaned his forehead on hers. "I love your slippers too."

She laughed. "What?"

"You said it yourself: 'Love me, love my slippers.' They can come too."

"Come where?"

"Wherever you want to live," he said excitedly. "We'll go to L.A. and open your business there . . . or there are many fine antiques to be had in Surrey and London and—"

"James, this is so sudden."

His dark eyes glowed with emotion. "You're wrong, Pussy-Kat, it's just that I've suddenly opened my eyes. Will you be my wife?"

Kat searched his face. "James, is this a permanent role?"

"Most definitely."

She smiled. "Then, yes."

His grin revealed both dimples as he lowered his mouth to hers. "Good—I've always wanted to get the girl."

THE EDITORS' CORNER

It's hard to believe that autumn is here! Soon Old Man Winter will be making his way down our paths, and we'll all be complaining about the cold weather instead of the oppressive heat. One thing you won't be complaining about is the Loveswept November lineup. And trust us, Old Man Winter doesn't stand a chance with these sexy men on the prowl!

Timing is everything, so they say, and Suzanne Brockmann proves the old adage true with her next LOVESWEPT, #858, **TIME ENOUGH FOR LOVE**. Chuck Della Croce has a problem. His time machine is responsible for a tragedy that has resulted in the deaths of hundreds. Thinking he can go back in time to literally save the world, Chuck ends up on Maggie Winthrop's doorstep. Maggie can't help but notice the stranger who's obnoxiously banging on her door, especially since he's naked as a jaybird! When he tells her he's from the future, she's ready to call the men in white coats, but something about him gives her pause. As Chuck explains his mission to prevent a disaster and save her life, Maggie must learn to accept that anything is possible. Suzanne Brockmann guides us in a timeless journey and persuades us to believe in the powers of destiny and second chances.

Eyes meeting across a crowded room, sexual tension building to a crescendo . . . *bam!*, you've got yourself a Loveswept! That certainly is the recipe conjured up in LOVESWEPT #859, **RELATIVE STRANGERS**, by Kathy Lynn Emerson. A ghost is lurking in the halls of Sinclair House, one who is anxious to reunite with her own true love. But first she must bring together the hearts of Lucas Sinclair and Corrie Ballantyne. Unfortunately, the two won't cooperate. Strange occurrences involving Corrie keep happening at Lucas's historic hotel, and he needs to get to the bottom of things before the place goes under. After seeing the ghosts of Lucas's ancestors, Corrie must decide if it's her own desire that draws her to him, or if it's the will of another. Can Corrie make peace with the past by unearthing hidden truths and soothing the unspoken sorrows of the man she will love forever? Kathy Lynn Emerson's exquisitely romantic ghost story is downright irresistible in both its sensuality and its mystery.

Trapped on an island with a hurricane on the loose, Trevor Fox and Jana Jenkins seek **SHELTER FROM THE STORM**, LOVESWEPT #860 by Maris Soule. Cursing a storm that had grounded all his charters, Trevor was only too glad to agree to lend a hand to the alluring seductress with the pouty lips.

Little did he know that his day would go from bad to worse, and from there to . . . well, whatever comes after that. Held at gunpoint, he is forced to fly to the Bahamas, and into the path of a hurricane. Jana Jenkins just wants to live a quiet, uneventful life, but when her stepbrother is kidnapped, Jana does what's necessary to save him—even if that includes dragging this brash pirate with a tarnished reputation along for the ride. Loveswept veteran Maris Soule knows there's nothing like a little danger to spice up the lives of a woman on the run and a man who enjoys the chase!

Dr. Kayla Davies learns just what will be her **ULTIMATE SURRENDER**, LOVESWEPT #861 by Jill Shalvis, an author who is penning her way into our hearts. When Kayla and her ex–brother-in-law, Ryan Scott, are summoned to the home of a beloved aunt, the two must make peace with their past and with each other. There's no love lost between the ruthless police detective and Kayla, but Ryan can't understand the fear he sees lurking in the depths of her blue eyes. As Kayla grows to know Ryan, she finds herself in the strange position of being both attracted and repelled by the man she once believed evil. Trapped in a web of old deceits, Ryan and Kayla struggle together to silence the ghosts of their past. But if Kayla dares to confess her dark secret, can Ryan find the strength to forgive? Writing with touching emotion and tender sensuality, Jill Shalvis once again proves that love can be a sweet victory over heartbreak.

Happy reading!

With warmest regards,

Susann Brailey   *Joy Abella*

Susann Brailey   Joy Abella

Senior Editor   Administrative Editor

P.S. Look for these Bantam women's fiction titles coming in November. From national bestselling author Kay Hooper comes **FINDING LAURA**, available in hardcover. A collector of mirrors, struggling artist Laura Sutherland stumbles across an antique hand mirror that lands her in the midst of the powerful Kilbourne family and a legacy of deadly intent. Leslie LaFoy makes her Bantam debut with **IT HAPPENED ONE NIGHT**. Allana Chapman was not prepared for the travel through time, and Kiervan des Marceaux must protect her in order to fulfill the prophecy and Allana's destiny as the Seer of the Find. Now available in paperback from *New York Times* bestselling author Sandra Brown is **HAWK O'TOOLE'S HOSTAGE**, a riveting contemporary romance about a woman who is held hostage by a desperate man . . . and a desperate desire. And immediately following this page, preview the Bantam women's fiction titles on sale in September.

For current information on Bantam's women's fiction, visit our new Web site, *Isn't It Romantic*, at the following address:

http://www.bdd.com/romance

Don't miss these extraordinary books
by your favorite Bantam authors!

On sale in September:

AFTER CAROLINE
by Kay Hooper

WHEN YOU WISH . . .
by Jane Feather, Patricia Coughlin, Sharon & Tom Curtis, Elizabeth Elliott, Patricia Potter, and Suzanne Robinson

THE BARGAIN
by Jane Ashford

THE CHALICE AND THE BLADE
by Glenna McReynolds

AFTER CAROLINE

BY KAY HOOPER

"Kay Hooper is a master storyteller."
—Tami Hoag

Two women who look enough alike to be twins. Both involved in car wrecks at the same time. One survives, one doesn't.

Now, plagued by a bewildering connection to a woman she never knew, driven by an urgent compulsion she doesn't understand, Joanna Flynn travels three thousand miles across the country to the picturesque town where Caroline McKenna lived—and mysteriously died. There Joanna will run into a solid wall of suspicion as she searches for the truth: Was Caroline's death an accident? Or was she the target of a killer willing to kill again?

"You're sure you're okay? No pain anywhere?"

"Not even a twinge." She looked past his shoulder to watch other motorists slipping and sliding down the bank toward her, and swallowed hard when she saw just how far her car had rolled. "My God. I should be dead, shouldn't I?"

Jim looked back and briefly studied the wide path of flattened brush and churned-up earth, then returned his gaze to her and smiled. "Like I said, this seems to be your lucky day."

Joanna looked once more at the car crumpled so snugly around her, and shivered. As close as she ever wanted to come . . .

Within five minutes, the rescue squad and paramedics arrived, all of them astonished but pleased to find her unhurt. Jim backed away to allow the rescue people room to work, joining the throng of onlookers scattered down the bank, and Joanna realized only then that she was the center of quite a bit of attention.

"I always wanted to be a star," she murmured.

The nearest paramedic, a brisk woman of about Joanna's age wearing a name badge that said E. Mallory, chuckled in response. "Word's gotten around that you haven't a scratch. Don't be surprised if the fourth estate shows up any minute."

Joanna was about to reply to that with another light comment, but before she could open her mouth, the calm of the moment was suddenly, terribly, shattered. There was a sound like a gunshot, a dozen voices screamed, *"Get back!"* and Joanna turned her gaze toward the windshield to see what looked like a thick black snake with a fiery head falling toward her out of the sky.

Then something slammed into her with the unbelievable force of a runaway train, and everything went black.

There was no sense of time passing, and Joanna didn't feel she had gone somewhere else. She felt . . . suspended, in a kind of limbo. Weightless, content, she drifted in a peaceful silence. She was waiting for something, she knew that. Waiting to find out something. The silence was absolute, but gradually the darkness began to abate, and she felt a gentle tug. She turned, or thought she did, and moved in the direction of the soft pull.

But almost immediately, she was released, drifting once more as the darkness deepened again. And she had a sudden sense that she was not alone, that someone shared the darkness with her. She felt a featherlight touch, so fleeting she wasn't at all sure of it, as though someone or something had brushed past her.

Don't let her be alone.

Joanna heard nothing, yet the plea was distinct in her mind, and the emotions behind it were nearly overwhelming. She tried to reach out toward that other, suffering presence, but before she could, something yanked at her sharply.

"Joanna? Joanna! Come on, Joanna, open your eyes!"

That summons was an audible one, growing louder as she felt herself pulled downward. She resisted for an instant, reluctant, but then fell in a rush until she felt the heaviness of her own body once more.

Instantly, every nerve and muscle she possessed seemed on fire with pain, and she groaned as she forced open her eyes.

A clear plastic cup over her face, and beyond it a circle of unfamiliar faces breaking into grins. And beyond *them* a clear blue summer sky decorated with fleecy white clouds. She was on the ground. What was she doing on the ground?

"She's back with us," one of the faces said back over his shoulder to someone else. "Let's get her on the stretcher." Then, to her, "You're going to be all right, Joanna. You're going to be just fine."

Joanna felt her aching body lifted. She watched dreamily as she floated past more faces. Then a vaguely familiar one appeared, and she saw it say something to her, something that sunk in only some time later as she rode in a wailing ambulance.

Definitely your lucky day. You almost died twice.

Her mind clearing by that time, Joanna could only agree with Jim's observation. How many people, after all, go through one near-death experience? Not many. Yet here she was, whole and virtually unharmed—if you discounted the fact that the only part of her body that didn't ache was the tip of her nose.

Still, she was very much alive, and incredibly grateful.

At the hospital, she was examined, soothed, and medicated. She would emerge from the day's incredible experiences virtually unscathed, the doctors told her. She had one burn mark on her right ankle where the electricity from the power line had arced between exposed metal and her flesh, and she'd be sore for a while both from the shock that had stopped her heart and from the later efforts to start it again.

She was a very lucky young lady and should suffer no lasting effects from what had happened to her; that was what they said.

But they were wrong. Because that was the night the dreams began.

WHEN YOU WISH . . .

BY JANE FEATHER, PATRICIA COUGHLIN, SHARON & TOM CURTIS, ELIZABETH ELLIOTT, PATRICIA POTTER, AND SUZANNE ROBINSON

To thine own wish be true. Do not follow the moth to the star.

So says the message in an exquisite green bottle. Is it a wish? A warning? A spell to cast over a lover? In six charming love stories, a mysterious bottle brings a touch of magic to the lives of all who possess it. . . .

The moon rode high against the soft blackness of the night sky. The great stones of the circle threw their shadows across the sleeping plain. The girl waited in the grove of trees. He had said he would come when the moon reached its zenith.

She shivered despite the warmth of the June night, drawing her woolen cloak about her. The massive pillars of Stonehenge held a menacing magic, even for one accustomed to the rites that took place within the sinister enclosure. The thought of venturing into the vast black space within the circle terrified her as it terrified all but the priests. It was forbidden ground.

Her ears were stretched for the sound of footsteps, although she knew that she would hear nothing as his sandaled feet slid over the moss of the grove. She stepped closer to the trunk of a poplar tree, then jumped back as she touched its encrustation of sacred mistletoe.

"Move into the moonlight."

Even though she'd been waiting for it, the soft command sent a thrill of fear shivering in her belly, curling her toes. She looked over her shoulder and saw him, shrouded in white, his hood pulled low over his head, only his eyes, pale blue in the darkness, gave life to the form.

The girl stepped out of the grove onto the moonlit plain. She felt him behind her. The priest who held the power of the Druid's Egg. She stopped, turned to face him. "Will you help me?"

"Are you certain you know what you're asking for?" His voice rasped, hoarse as if he'd been shouting for hours. The pale blue eyes burned in their deep sockets.

She nodded. "I am certain." With a sudden movement, she shook off her hood. Her hair cascaded down her back, a silver river in the moonlight. "Will the magic work?"

A smile flashed across his eyes and he reached out to touch her hair. "It has the power of desires and dreams."

"To make them come true?" Her voice was anxious, puzzled.

He said nothing, but drew from beneath his cloak a thick-bladed knife. "Are you ready?"

The girl swallowed, nodded her head. She turned her back to the priest. She felt him take her hair at the nape of her neck. She felt the knife sawing through the thick mass, silvered by the moon. She felt it part beneath the blade. And then she stood shorn, the night air cold on her bare neck. "Now you will give it to me?"

He was winding the hank of hair around his hand and didn't answer as he reveled in the richness of the payment. The hair of a maiden had many useful properties but it was a potent sacrifice that few young virgins were voluntarily prepared to make. He opened a leather pouch at his waist and carefully deposited the shining mass inside, before taking out an object of green glass. It lay on his flat palm.

She looked closely at it. A green glass bottle with a chased silver top. Vertical banks of chased silver flowed down the bottle from the stopper, like liquid mercury. There was something inside it. She could see the shape in the neck behind the glowing glass. Would it work? It had to work. Only the magic of a man who held the power of the Druid's Egg could enable her to make the right decision.

She reached out and touched it tentatively with her fingertip. "The spell is within?"

"You will read it within."

"What must I do? Must I open it in a certain way? Read it in a certain way?"

"You will read it as it is meant to be read." The smile was there again as he took her hand and placed the bottle on her plam. "As it is meant to be read for you," he added.

Her fingers closed over the bottle. She frowned, wondering what he could mean. A spell was a spell, surely. It could only be read one way.

When she looked up, the priest had gone.

The Druid's Egg was hatched by several serpents laboring together. When hatched it was held in the air by their hissing. The man who had given her the spell had caught the egg as it danced on the serpent's venom. He had caught it and escaped the poison himself. Such a man . . . such a priest . . . had the power to do anything.

Holding the bottle tightly in her fist, the girl turned her back on the stone pillars. She tried to walk but soon was running across the plain toward the village nestled in a fold of land beside the river that flowed to the sea. She had never seen the sea, only heard tales of vast blueness that disappeared into the sky. But the river flowing between sloping banks was her friend.

She sat down on the bank outside the village and with trembling fingers opened the bottle. A scrap of leather, carefully rolled, lay inside. She drew it out, unfurled it, held it up to the bright moonlight.

Runes were scratched into the leather at the top, and at the sight of the magic symbols her heart leaped. She hadn't sold her hair for nothing. Here was the incantation she had bought. She squinted at the strange marks and wondered what she was to do with them. Only when she turned the leather over did she see the writing in legible strokes inked onto the leather.

"To thine own wish be true. Do not follow the moth to the star."

The girl stared in disbelieving dismay. What did it mean? It told her nothing. There was nothing magic about those words. She looked again at the runes and knew in her bones that they would add nothing to the message. They were decoration for a simple truth. She thrust the scrap of leather back into the bottle and corked it.

Be true to her own wish. Was it telling her she must face the consequences of her desires? If she wished for the stars, she would burn like the moth at the candle.

Slowly, she stood up. She held her hand over the swift flowing water and opened it. The little bottle dropped, was caught by the current and whisked away toward the distant sea. As distant as the stars.

The choice was still hers to make. The road still branched before her. She had sold her hair for the druid's power and she was left, as always, with only her own.

"Jane Ashford is an exceptional talent."
—*Rendezvous*

THE BARGAIN

BY JANE ASHFORD

It's more than ridiculous, it's damned embarrassing and inconvenient . . . for a scientist with his reputation to be called in to get rid of a ghost. But when the prince regent summons Lord Alan Gresham to London to solve the mystery of a haunting, he has no choice. At least the task shouldn't take much time. He will uncover the perpetrators of the hoax and then return with speed to his experiments. Or so Gresham thinks, until he finds his calm, logical investigation disrupted by a maddeningly forthright beauty. Ariel Harding has her own reasons for wanting to catch the ghost. Yet when she slips into Carlton House uninvited, she never dreams she'll end up locked in a closet with an arrogant, opinionated, yet undeniably attractive scientist . . . or that she'll wind up making a perilous bargain with the very same man. They agree to exchange information—and nothing more. But neither plans on the most confounding of scientific occurrences: the breathless chemistry of desire.

"No, I do not wish to stroll with you in the garden," the girl said. "I have told you so a dozen times. I don't wish to be rude, but please go away."

The man grasped her arm, his fingers visibly digging into her flesh. He tried to pull her along with him through the crowd.

"I'll scream," said the girl, rather calmly. "I can scream very loudly. My singing teacher said I have an extraordinary set of lungs. Though an unreliable grasp of pitch," she added with regretful honesty.

Her companion ignored this threat until the girl actually opened her mouth and drew in a deep preparatory breath. Then, with a look around at the crowd and a muttered oath, he dropped her arm. "Witch," he said.

" 'Double, double toil and trouble,' " she replied pertly.

The man frowned.

" 'Fire, burn; and, cauldron, bubble,' " she added.

His frown became a scowl.

"Something of toad, eye of newt . . . oh, I forget the rest." She sounded merely irritated at her lapse of memory.

The man backed away a few steps.

"There's blood in it somewhere," she told herself. She made an exasperated sound. "I used to know the whole thing by heart."

Her would-be ravisher took to his heels. The girl shook out her skirts and tossed her head in satisfaction.

His interest definitely caught, Alan examined this unusual creature more closely. She was small—the top of her head did not quite reach his shoulder—but the curves of her form were not at all childlike. The bodice of her pale green gown was admirably filled and it draped a lovely line of waist and hip. Her skin glowed like ripe peaches against her glossy brown hair. He couldn't see whether her eyes had any resemblance to forest pools, but her lips were mesmerizing—very full and beautifully shaped. The word "luscious" occurred to him, and he immediately rejected it as nonsense. What the devil was he doing, he wondered? He wasn't a man to be beguiled by physical charms, or to waste his time on such maunderings. Still, he was having trouble tearing his eyes away from her when it was brought home to him that she had noticed him.

"No, I do not wish to go with you into another

room," she declared, meeting his gaze squarely. "Or into the garden, or out to your carriage. I do not require an escort home. Nor do I need someone to tell me how to go on or to 'protect' me." She stared steadily up at him, not looking at all embarrassed.

"What are you doing here?" he couldn't resist asking her.

"That is none of your affair. What are *you* doing here?"

Briefly, Alan wondered what she would think if he told her. He would enjoy hearing her response, he realized. But of course he couldn't reveal his supposed "mission."

A collective gasp passed over the crowd, moving along the room like wind across a field of grain. Alan turned quickly. This was what he had been waiting for through the interminable hours and days. There! He started toward the sweeping staircase that adorned the far end of the long room, pushing past knots of guests transfixed by the figure that stood in the shadows atop it.

On the large landing at the head of the stairs the candles had gone out—or been blown out, Alan amended. In the resulting pool of darkness, floating above the sea of light in the room, was a figure out of some sensational tale. It was a woman, her skin bone-white, her hair a deep chestnut. She wore an antique gown of yellow brocade, the neck square cut, the bodice tight above a long full skirt. Alan knew, because he had been told, that this invariably was her dress when she appeared, and that it was the costume she had worn onstage to play Lady Macbeth.

Sound reverberated through the room—the clanking of chains—as Alan pushed past the guests, who remained riveted by the vision before them. The figure seemed to hover a foot or so above the floor. The space between the hem of its gown and the stair landing was a dark vacancy. Its eyes were open, glassy and fixed, effectively dead-looking. Its hands and arms were stained with gore.

A bloodcurdling scream echoed down the stairs. Then a wavering, curiously guttural voice pronounced the word "justice" very slowly, three times. The figure's mouth had not moved during any of this, Alan noted.

He had nearly reached the foot of the stairs when a female guest just in front of him threw up her arms and crumpled to the floor in a faint. Alan had to swerve and slow to keep from stepping on her, and as he did so, something struck him from behind, upsetting his balance and nearly knocking him down. "What the devil?" he said, catching himself and moving on even as he cast a glance over his shoulder. To his astonishment, he found that the girl he had encountered a moment ago was right on his heels. He didn't have time to wonder what she thought she was doing. "Stay out of my way," he commanded, and lunged for the stairs.

In one of the most original and stunning hardcover debuts of the season, Glenna McReynolds brings historical romance readers the experience they've been waiting for: a novel of dark magic, stirring drama, and fierce passion that weaves a wondrous, unbreakable spell . . .

THE CHALICE
AND THE BLADE
BY GLENNA MCREYNOLDS

The place is twelfth-century Wales, a land of forbidding castles and ferocious knights, sacred prophesies and unholy betrayals. Deep in the caverns below the towers of Carn Merioneth, dragon nests await the arrival of one who holds the key to an ancient legacy. She is Ceridwen, daughter of a Druid priestess, unaware of her immense power—until fate leads her to a feared sorcerer. Dain Lavrans knows he has no magic, only the secrets of medicine he uncovered in the Crusades. But with the appearance of Ceridwen, he will finally behold true—and terrifying—magic, for there are many who seek to use the maiden to unlock the mystery of the dragons. Now a battle of epic proportion is about to take place. At its center stand Ceridwen and Dain, struggling to escape the snares set by friend and foe alike, while discovering that neither can resist the love that promises to bind them forever.

On sale in October:

FINDING LAURA
by Kay Hooper

HAWK O'TOOLE'S HOSTAGE
by Sandra Brown

IT HAPPENED ONE NIGHT
by Leslie LaFoy

DON'T MISS THESE FABULOUS
BANTAM WOMEN'S FICTION TITLES